Medway COUNCIL

LIBRARY	WALDERSLADE LIBRARY
	HOOK MEADOW
	KING GEORGE ROAD
	WALDERSLADE
TELEPHONE	CHATHAM
	KENT ME5 0TZ
	01634 861531

17. 09.		14.
		71-LANGR
	29. DEC	15.
		03 JAN 2018
	31. JAN 11.	
08.	16. MAR 11.	26 JAN 2018
MAR 09.		
22-5-09	8 MAY	

Books should be returned or renewed by the last date stamped above

MEDWAY LIBRARIES
9560000206793

DEVOTED SISTERS

Alison Buck

An Alnpete Book

Devoted Sisters
First published in Great Britain by Alnpete Press, 2006
An imprint of Alnpete Limited

Copyright © Alison Buck, 2006
All rights reserved

The right of Alison Buck to be identified as the author of this work has been asserted in accordance with sections 77 and 78 of the Copyright, Designs and Patents Act 1988. No part of this publication may be reproduced, stored in a retrieval system or transmitted in any form, or by any means (electronic, mechanical, telepathic, or otherwise) without the prior written permission of the copyright owner.

Alnpete Press, PO Box 757
Dartford, Kent
DA2 7TQ

www.alnpetepress.co.uk

A CIP catalogue record for this book is available from the British Library

ISBN 0-9552206-1-0
EAN 978-0-9552206-1-6

Condition of Sale
This book is sold subject to the condition that it shall not, by way of trade or otherwise, be lent, re-sold, hired out or otherwise circulated in any form of binding or cover other than that in which it is published and without a similar condition including this condition being imposed on the subsequent purchaser.

This book is copyright under the Berne Convention.
Alnpete Press & Leaf Design is a trademark of Alnpete Limited

This book is a work of fiction. All names, characters, places and events are either a product of the author's fevered imagination or are used fictitiously. Any resemblance to actual events, places, or people living or dead, is purely coincidental.

Printed by Antony Rowe Limited

For Peter

1

The long, gentle day was almost over, the low evening sun almost gone.

But before dusk settled its stillness on the house, the softly blazing clouds parted briefly. For those few moments, the old red brick wall glowed warm again and the blistered paint of the window frame came back to life, gilded to fantastical baroque beauty. Then the moment passed, the clouds slipped back across the sun and the golden touch began to fade.

Beyond the window's dusty glass, the last drowsy shaft of light slanted across the quiet room and settled on the smiling face of an old woman. At ease in her armchair, feeling the warmth of the last light of the day, she stilled her hands and let her knitting come to rest on her lap. She held her breath a moment then sighed, a long, comfortable sigh. Had May been asked how she felt, at that moment, she would have described the joy of glorious summers in her early childhood; picnics in fields of swaying grasses and skies of the dazzling cloudless blue that filled your soul to overflowing. Mother laughing, braiding flowers into their hair. Everyone smiling, golden, all cares forgotten in the embrace of balmy summer air. It was the delight of bare feet running on hot dusty earth, the freedom and the laughter of childhood, all summoned in an instant as the fading sunlight touched her face, the intervening years fallen completely away.

Utterly content, May sat entranced, watching dancing motes swirling silently in the pale shaft of light; continuous, aimless motion while everything else in the room was at rest.

Sunset had always been a special time of day, even from May's earliest memories. She remembered she had sat watching sundown on an evening just like this, a lifetime ago. Mother had come to speak to her and May could, even now, picture the glowing halo that the sun had made of the hair framing her mother's face. May was so fascinated that she didn't listen to what she was being told. Her tearful mother had to repeat herself and finally grasp the little girl's shoulders to break the spell and gently shake her to attentiveness. Father was missing. Mother hoped that they would hear news of him soon, but for now May had to be a good little girl and pray as hard as she could for his safe return. But even as she nodded gravely, promising that she would pray really, really hard for Father, May's mind had still been focused on the prettiness of the light on her mother's hair.

Over the years, May had occasionally recalled and regretted her childish inattention, but she could only have been three or four at the time and, spellbound by the wonderful evening light in her mother's hair, she simply hadn't grasped the importance of what was being said. She hadn't understood.

Dabbing at her eyes with her handkerchief, May smiled again and gently shook her head. She had always been easily confused, so often misunderstanding what was going on; but, throughout her life, she had been fortunate in having people around her who cared for her and loved her. Especially Lizzie. She always had Lizzie, her elder sister, the sensible one. Lizzie understood how things were; always knew what had to be done. She was bossy of course, but that was just her way. She had always cared for May, her baby sister.

It had been on another such warm and golden evening, some years later, that May had sat out on the verandah on the day that Father finally came home from the war. He had been a prisoner in a camp, but now his war was over. Mother had been given just a few hours notice that he was coming home to them and the house was in uproar while preparations were made. Everyone else was excited. Lizzie and their brother, Frank, hurriedly made a banner from scraps of stiff blue wallpaper. It read, 'Welcome home Father' and it flapped crisply in the breeze, above the front door. Frank and Lizzie waited at the gate all afternoon, keen to get the first glimpse of their father. But May chose to hide away on the verandah at the back of the house. So much younger than the others, she no longer remembered her father at all. She had no memory of any adult man in the house and the prospect of a stranger being thrust into her world was quite terrifying.

But gradually, as she crouched in a corner, the comforting warmth of the setting sun calmed her. She began to feel protected, safe. The garden darkened and moths came to the verandah, drawn by the light from the kitchen window. Watching them, oblivious to the passing of several hours, May became so enchanted that she didn't notice the sounds of activity at the front of the house when her father finally arrived. The verandah had been in near total darkness when Mother came searching and found May kneeling by the window, marvelling at a tiny moth resting on her finger. Despite May's pleading, Mother insisted she leave the moth behind. Mother led her into the very room in which May was sitting now where, then, Father had been waiting.

That meeting with her father was a strangely silent and stilted affair. Deeply affected by his imprisonment, he would never again be the lively, loving man who had been swept away to war. Father and daughter were foreign to each other; complete unknowns. At a loss to know what else to do, May simply stared up at this stranger's face. While her father, similarly ill at ease, looked down at her from across the room with an equal lack of recognition and with such apparent coldness that May struggled in panic, like someone drowning, when her mother gently urged her to go to him. Neither father nor daughter said a word.

Eager to get away, May ran from the room as soon as her mother released her hand. Subsequently, as was to become her habit when dealing with any of life's unpleasantness, May had put the encounter out of her mind and she had recalled it on very few occasions in all the time since. In fact, the only thing of importance that May consciously carried with her from that momentous day of her father's return to his family was an abiding fascination with and love of moths.

The light had now faded, reducing the dancing motes to invisibility and May let her eyes close, her mouth a contented smile. But the peace was rudely shattered when, with sudden noisy activity, Lizzie thrust open the door, snapped on the light and marched into the room.

Unlike her more frail and dependent younger sister, Lizzie took great pride in her own relative strength. She stood erect and had about her an air of purposeful fierceness, always busy, always watchful, always alert. She refused to let the years weaken her and she had far too much to do to allow herself to slide into a gentle old age and inactivity, as had her younger sister.

Lizzie strode over to the window and pulled the blinds down.

"For goodness' sake, May, don't leave the blinds open after dark. I've told you before, the light in here lets people see in and you never know who's out there just watching for a house that's worth breaking into."

With a resigned sigh, May adjusted her glasses on her nose and picked up her knitting once more.

"It's no good you sighing like that. You won't be so calm when some young thug breaks in and kills us in our beds."

"The sun has only just gone down Lizzie. I'm sure thugs, young or old, would wait till it's a good deal darker before they go out prowling."

Not for the first time, Lizzie had the nagging suspicion that her sister was mocking her. It was too much! May didn't take any of Lizzie's concerns seriously. Never had. May lived from day to day in a cosy fantasy, her only activities: knitting, breadmaking and gardening; her only interest, those blessed moths. Comfortably cocooned in her safe, familiar surroundings, May had no understanding of the bigger world that lay beyond.

Lizzie on the other hand had to deal with that dangerous outside world and she felt the burden of responsibility increasingly heavy on her shoulders. They were alone now, just the two of them, and Lizzie had promised Mother that she would always look after her little sister. Though they were both now old women, Lizzie still felt herself bound by that promise.

Lizzie had never married; how could she when there was always May to care for? Perhaps because of this, their brother Frank had become her closest friend. He had been privy to all Lizzie's secret hopes and dreams. Long ago, when May had simply been 'the baby', Lizzie had been a fearless tomboy: playing soldiers and climbing trees with Frank and his schoolmates. She and Frank had shared such adventures, such wonderful times.

Now it was Lizzie's turn to sigh. She missed Frank so very much.

He had grown to become the sort of man that Lizzie might have looked for as a husband. Indeed for years she and Frank had been partners, in their shared life here in this house. Sadly their comfortable rhythm and routine had ended abruptly when Frank met a girl at work, fell hopelessly in love and, all too soon, left home to marry.

Lizzie had never warmed to Frank's wife, Vera and while she magnanimously conceded that some of her reaction was jealousy, there was no escaping from the inexplicability of Frank's choice; it was abundantly clear to Lizzie that Vera was silly, weak and even more irritatingly foolish than May. Try as she might, and she did try a little, Lizzie could never understand what Frank saw in Vera. Why was he always so protective of her, giving in to her every whim? Why were Vera's wishes always paramount? Lizzie felt her beloved brother had been stolen away, wrenched from her life.

After Vera's arrival, Lizzie and Frank had precious little time or opportunity to talk as they once had. On one treasured occasion though, on Christmas Eve, Vera had retired early to bed and Lizzie and Frank had been able to talk together, in earnest confidence, far into the quiet hours of the night. Lizzie had remembered that stolen conversation for the rest of her life. Frank told her of his love for Vera and his hopes for their future together. With tears in his beautiful eyes, he also confided that Vera was apparently too delicate for the demands of pregnancy, so his long-held wish to become a father would never be realised. It seemed that Vera was similarly too fragile to cook or manage a home and Frank would have to work extra hours to pay for a cook and a housekeeper. Lizzie was unconvinced; Vera was slim certainly, but frail, no. Also it seemed strange to Lizzie that Vera's delicate constitution was sufficiently robust to allow frequent visits to the beauty parlour and equally frequent shopping trips, during which Vera purchased the exquisite tailored suits she so loved. Exploiting Frank's inexperience and trusting nature, Vera had him dancing entirely to her tune, and Lizzie grew to hate her for it.

Just before dawn on that long ago Christmas morning, Lizzie had looked into Frank's sad, lovely eyes, lit solely by the dim glow of the lamp on the table between them. In that otherwise darkened room, his face was luminous with his tragic infatuation for the undeserving Vera. Frank had paused, waiting for Lizzie to speak, wanting her reaction; wanting her approval. If ever she had had a chance to save him from Vera, it was in that moment, in the dark silence of the sleeping house. Moments passed and time seemed to slow, awaiting Lizzie's response. But how could she say what she so desperately wanted to? Frank loved Vera with an all-consuming surrender of himself. To tell him how truly ordinary and lacking in merit the woman was would have been to break him, or forever shatter the wonderful friendship that he and Lizzie had all their lives enjoyed. In the lengthening silence, Lizzie had to choose a future, either sharing Frank with Vera, or losing him to Vera completely and probably forever.

Lizzie chose. She looked across at Frank's open, trusting eyes and forced her own face to convey both her love, which was intensely real, and an understanding, which was utterly beyond her. Even as she mouthed the supportive and sympathetic platitudes, her mind had been filled with doubts and questions. Above all, how could it be possible that she was losing her beloved brother in such a way, to such a dull and feeble person? And how could Frank not see what a burdensome, utterly worthless woman Vera really was?

Frank and Vera were married just two years. But it wasn't poor, 'fragile' Vera who succumbed. It was Frank. He had died, quickly and unexpectedly, from a haemorrhage in his brain.

Lizzie's heart had been broken then and she always felt she had never truly recovered from the shock of his death. In her mind, she could see still Frank the boy; laughing, sharing some silly joke, cheering the gang with his infectious enthusiasm, encouraging everyone to join him in a childhood of fantastical adventures. She could see also the caring and gentle young man who quietly eased the burden from Father's shoulders, working hard to provide for them all. Eventually, as Father became ill and Mother slowly faded, Frank had become the heart of the family, a source of comfort and strength for them all. Then all too soon and with no warning, he was gone.

Even now after so many years, not a day passed without Lizzie thinking of him and missing their special friendship. Growing older without him, she had felt the loss of his strength and his reassuring presence ever more keenly with the passing years. He would have protected both her and May. With him, Lizzie would have been safe from the many terrors that populated the outside world of her imaginings.

Less than a year after Frank's death, Vera had married a shoe salesman from Rochester. To Lizzie's immense relief, she and Vera had never so much as exchanged a Christmas card since.

Maybe Vera was dead by now, Lizzie mused, with no little amusement.

But the pleasure was short-lived and her half smile quickly turned to a scowl, at the sudden, awful thought of Frank and Vera being reunited in death.

2

After what had been a wet and dismal winter, the late spring weather was wonderfully warm and today, to her surprise, Lizzie found herself enjoying the walk back from town. She still held her purse close to her chest and she gripped the handle of her small shopping bag so tightly that she was painfully aware of the re-stitched seams of her gloves pressing into the base of her thumb. But, in spite of her accustomed caution, Lizzie allowed herself to walk a little more slowly than was usual today.

On the corner opposite the school she even paused for a moment to smile at the children playing in the yard. What a delightful picture they were, scampering about and how odd that she'd not noticed them playing there before. But then, she was always so busy. She had things to do and she had responsibilities; no time to waste in idleness. Still, it was good to see the little ones enjoying themselves in this glorious sunshine. Lizzie smiled again, then amazed herself by waving her hand and nodding. Bemused, the children didn't respond in kind but simply stared back at the old woman until, feeling rather foolish, Lizzie turned away and resumed her more usual, brisk pace. However, once around the next corner she again slowed down and permitted herself a moment or two of self-indulgence. The weather was truly wonderful.

Brilliant, gaudy sunlight washed over everything, bringing to life new and welcome colour. It was good just to be alive on a day like this, and it was as if Lizzie was experiencing it all for the first time in years.

But before the feeling of well-being overwhelmed her completely, Lizzie stopped herself. She had to come to her senses. She must be careful. Even on as glorious a day as today, she must stay on her guard.

Lizzie glanced around. She knew there were muggers everywhere these days, and so few decent folk around during the working day that anything could happen and no one would see, no one would know. She frowned. How much the town had changed. It had been so very different when she was a child.

Mother and Father had moved into their house when it was newly built and all three children had been born there. Her parents' new friends had, like them, been young and full of hope, happy to be raising their families in so perfect a town. Everything was new, freshly painted and bright. Every day had been sunny and vibrant, like today. Everything was alive and spirits were high with an unshakable confidence in an ever brighter tomorrow. Back then, they had believed that anything was possible. Everyone was determined to improve their lives and put the terrible anxieties of the Depression behind them for good. Those had been optimistic times. Wonderfully happy times.

Lizzie remembered the large tree that had once stood at the corner of Oak Avenue. Commemorated now only in the name of the road, it had then been the centre of activity for all the lively young spirits in the neighbourhood, a focus for their imaginations. She and Frank and all his friends had climbed up into that tree and imagined it a galleon, a castle or a Wild West stage coach. They had ridden that tree into so many wonderful adventures.

'But,' she thought sadly, 'Nothing stays the same forever.'

The tree had long since gone and the whole area was now paved over. It had been a lifetime ago, but Lizzie had never again been so joyous and carefree as she had been then. Life had promised so much. The road ahead could have taken a person anywhere and Frank's happy gang had had such great dreams.

Lizzie couldn't help but smile as she remembered Billy Pierce, an earnest little boy with a bowl-trimmed thatch of straw coloured hair. Being so slight and yet heedless of any danger, Billy had always climbed higher than anyone else, spreading his arms wide to catch the wind far above, in the swaying upper branches. Billy was going to be a famous flyer. He was going to fly to every country and every city in the whole, wide world. Just you wait and see.

But, as is the way of things, time had passed and Billy's wonderful dream had gradually been bleached clean away in that harshest of lights; the reality that lights the adult world; a reality of unforgiving limitations and closed horizons. Billy apparently had neither the brains nor the eyesight to train as a pilot and the one and only time he had ever travelled in an airplane he'd been sick as a dog. Billy learnt to bury his dreams as people do and he'd been running the hardware store for over thirty years now, as his father and uncle had done for thirty years before him. Though his thatch had thinned and long ago turned a frosty grey, his smile was as ready as it ever had been, but with the loss of his dream his eyes had lost forever that wonderful sparkle of childhood. Billy had accepted the passing of his dreams with affable equanimity and no self-pity, but he had often joked with Frank that things would have been different if his father had owned a grocery rather than a hardware store. How much better his eyesight would have been if he'd just eaten enough carrots! Frank had always laughed along with his old friend and Lizzie, remembering, was smiling now. But her smile soon faded; Lizzie realised that she was thinking of Frank again and the wound of that loss would never heal.

'We all have to give up on our dreams', she mused, 'Or maybe, if we don't act on them, they give up on us.'

She pulled herself back to the present, lifted her chin in an air of defiance and marched down the narrow track towards the isolated house.

Wheezing slightly, Lizzie climbed the steps to the front door, opened her bag and felt inside for her keys, all the while keeping a careful watch around her. After one final, almost furtive, look over her shoulder, she turned her attention to the lock and in one swift motion unlocked and opened the door, slid quickly inside and pushed it closed behind her. She stood for a while, her back resting against the door, as she regained her composure.

How she hated that moment's distraction when she had to unlock the door. One of the greater of her many fears was that someone would attack her then, jumping at her from behind, in those few seconds while her attention was on locating the keyhole and opening the door. It didn't matter at all that this was the middle of a bright and sunny day in a quiet, uneventful suburb. The fear was constant and very real to Lizzie. She always needed a few moments to recover.

Eventually, drawing in a deep breath, she straightened up from the door and walked towards the kitchen. She put the bags on the table and started to put away the food. Closing the door of the refrigerator, she glanced up. The back door was ajar. Lizzie froze in a moment of indecision, then, leaving the rest of the food, she moved cautiously around the table, behind the half-open door.

Biting her lip, she peered out through its small frosted window.

"Dear God!"

As May's face popped up on the other side of the pane, Lizzie shrieked.

"What are you doing jumping up like that? You gave me such a shock."

May opened the door fully and smiled indulgently at her sister.

"I didn't jump, dear. And I've only been in the garden, picking some greens. There's no need to be alarmed."

"No need? What do you mean? You left the door unlocked again. How many times do I have to tell you? Always lock the door behind you when you go out. Someone could sneak in here while you're out in the vegetable patch and the first you'd know about it would be when you came back in here to find everything you love broken or stolen or worse."

"Worse?" May asked.

Lizzie didn't enlarge on what 'worse' might involve. She was calmer now, recovering from the shock and May didn't need to know what sort of people there were out there. She didn't need to know the sort of dreadful crimes that were committed every day against defenceless old ladies just like her. They had no television or radio in the house and no newspapers delivered, so May simply had no idea.

Lizzie knew though. Twice a week, on Mondays and Fridays, her short visits to buy their food and pay any bills allowed her to find out all she needed to know about the world outside. On a Monday, at the town's library, Lizzie would first return May's library book and take out another unlikely romance or adventure for her, picked at random from the shelves of well-thumbed paperbacks. That done, Lizzie would go into the reference section to read all the newspapers from cover to cover, except the sports sections, which she dismissed as being nothing more than a frivolous waste of newsprint. On alternate Fridays, the library was closed, but Lizzie still kept up with events by reading all the headlines and front pages on display at the news stand; she had to keep herself informed. It was her job to protect May from all that wickedness, but it would be so much easier if May would, for once, listen to her instructions.

As they cleared the dishes after their supper that evening, May managed to cause her poor sister additional anxiety.

"Lizzie, I think I'll go outside and sit a little while. I'd like to see if there are any interesting moths in the garden tonight."

Lizzie's reply was brusque.

"Don't be silly May, you can just as easily watch for them at the window. They're moths for goodness' sake. Just leave a lamp outside on the verandah and they'll come to you."

That, she thought, would settle the matter. But May was not so easily dissuaded.

"It's not the same through glass Lizzie. You only see their underside and not their pretty wings."

"They don't have pretty wings, May, that's butterflies."

"Oh no, Lizzie, moths are such delicate little creatures. They may not be as flamboyant as butterflies, but I like to think they have their own exquisite beauty."

Lizzie arched an eyebrow. May's occasional use of these fancy and quite unnecessary terms caused her sister great irritation. Flamboyant! Exquisite! What was wrong with simply saying they weren't as 'colourful' as butterflies? It seemed to Lizzie that May's highfalutin words hinted at a depth of learning completely at odds with her usual air of child-like confusion. Over their years together, and increasingly in recent months, Lizzie had found herself wondering if May's silliness was affectation. But why would anyone pretend to be so helpless and foolish? Why would May do it? What did it gain her?

Nothing.

It gained her nothing because it wasn't pretence and it shamed Lizzie that she suspected her sister of such deceit.

Time and again, Lizzie had argued herself to this same conclusion and, every time, she had then reproved herself for ever thinking her sister devious. May was just the way she was and always had been and that was that.

Lizzie brought herself back to the conversation,

"I've already locked up for the night," she said, "You'll have to watch them at the window."

May was disgruntled, but accepting.

"Well, tomorrow, please don't lock up so early, because I really want to go out on the verandah to watch for the moths."

For a moment Lizzie was tempted to say something non-committal that would leave May with the hope of going outside the following night, but she determined instead to be honest.

"No, May. You mustn't go outside after dark. I've explained it all before."

"But I always used to go out looking for moths after dark. I even used to stay out all night sometimes. Don't you remember?"

"Of course I remember. But that was then and this is now."

May frowned, quite baffled by this bald statement of the obvious. Lizzie realised that May might never have come across the expression before. Lizzie herself had only ever encountered it within the pages of newspapers.

"It means that times have changed. Things are not as they used to be."

"Oh I know they're not, dear." said May, her frown melting away. With a reassuring smile that put Lizzie in mind of a child wise beyond her years, May patted Lizzie's hand, "Nothing stays the same forever."

"That's funny," said Lizzie.

"What is, dear?"

"I was thinking just the very same thing earlier today," said Lizzie wistfully, "when I was walking past where the oak tree used to be."

"Which oak tree, dear?"

Lizzie shrugged and made no reply. The tree, of course, held no special place in May's memories. She had been too young; she'd never joined the tree climbers and shared their adventures. But maybe she had her own dreams.

As Lizzie looked into her sister's pretty hazel eyes, so less weary and blood shot than her own, she thought 'You don't change, do you May?' Maybe, of all the people Lizzie had ever known, May, who lived apart from the world with its limitations and ugliness, whose legs were brittle with arthritis, was the only one who had managed to hold onto her childlike self. Perhaps May hadn't given up on her dreams.

But nothing stays the same forever.

3

May was angry.

"You locked up early again on purpose. After I asked you not to, you locked up early again. It really is too bad."

Having said her piece, May turned her head towards the wall, her soft, lined face set in the petulant sulk of a child. Lizzie had to be made to realise how unfair this was and so, until she relented, May would neither look at her nor speak to her again. This time she was determined.

But Lizzie was equally determined, for her part, to make May understand that she, Lizzie, really did know best. Venturing outside after dark was madness; anything could happen.

Such determination, on both sides, made for a tense silence in the minutes that followed.

Eventually, in spite of her earlier resolve, May tried again.

"I'm not asking you to go out, Lizzie dear," she said, "You can stay indoors if you're frightened."

"Frightened? I'm not frightened." Lizzie's answer had been too quick, her voice a little too high, but she persisted, "How dare you say I'm frightened?"

May entirely failed to read the confirmation of fear in Lizzie's apparently outraged indignation. She looked fleetingly hopeful.

"Then come out with me, please Lizzie. Come and help me look for the moths. They are so beautiful."

"Beautiful? Rubbish! For the last time, you must not go out after dark."

"But-"

"No. No buts. You don't know what the world out there is like these days. It's just too dangerous. There are so many strange people around. And, even if there weren't, imagine what would happen if you tripped over something or had a fall. What would happen then?"

"Well I suppose I'd just have to lie there until you came and found me, dear. But it's not so big a garden. I'm sure you'd find me in good time."

"Thank you! So I'd have to go out in the dark to find you would I? And meanwhile, someone could break into the house, or I could fall as well, or someone could attack both of us and there'd be no one left to raise the alarm then, would there?"

May tried another tack,

"Well, how would it be if you stayed in the house and, if you thought I'd been out for too long, you could raise the alarm."

"How? How would I do that when we don't have a telephone?"

"Well, for goodness sake, Lizzie, let's get a telephone. I've always said we should have one."

"Money doesn't grow on trees, you know. And there's the problem of nuisance calls." Lizzie ignored May's quizzical frown, "And, worse than that, thieves call you on your telephone to check if you're in, so that they can break in when you're out."

May was exasperated.

"But we never are out Lizzie. Even if the thieves did call, we'd always be here. Don't you see, dear, we'd be quite safe."

But Lizzie had had enough. In time-honoured fashion, the argument ended with Lizzie invoking May's promise to their mother: that she would always listen to Lizzie, who in return would always look after her.

"I've made my decision and that's final. You promised Mother, so please let that be an end to it."

Lizzie may have had the last word but on this occasion, unusually, it was May who walked away from the argument first, pushing herself to her feet and walking stiffly from the room in resentful silence. It was clear that May was angry and upset, but Lizzie was sure she would feel herself bound by the promise she had made to their mother. May would never break a promise.

Alone in the room now, Lizzie sank, exhausted, into an armchair. Her heart was beating uncomfortably fast and, unsettled, she turned the argument over in her mind. How could May have accused her of being frightened? If she were frightened she wouldn't go out to town every week would she? And it was always she who went out on all the errands. Never May. Frightened indeed!

Lizzie couldn't acknowledge the truth even to herself. She was more than simply frightened: she was terrified. The possibility of having to go out into the pitch dark garden to rescue May was appalling. At the very thought of it Lizzie felt her chest tighten and her hands begin to tremble. But if the need arose she knew she would have to go, terror and danger notwithstanding. She had promised Mother that she would always look after May, and she was bound to that promise as May was to hers. But to be outside and surrounded by the all-concealing darkness. Oh God, the very idea set her heart racing again.

But Lizzie deluded herself that it wasn't fear on her own behalf, but rather it was fear for May's safety. May was too remote from the world to understand the possible depths of its depravity. She must be made to understand that, in matters like these, she had to listen to a wiser head.

May was an innocent.

It had never once occurred to Lizzie that she might explain something of the world to May. To do that would be to destroy the innocence that made May so special. Lizzie felt, as she always had, that she must be the wall protecting May's bright, childlike openness from the wickedness lurking just beyond the safe embrace of their home. Only rarely, and then only in the lonely early hours of the night, did Lizzie let herself imagine what this ignorance might one day mean for May. What would happen if Lizzie were to die first, leaving May all alone? In those anxious midnight hours, feeling utterly hopeless and alone, Lizzie would stare into this shadowy abyss of future possibility. She didn't know what she should do. She had no answer. She just had to hang on. She had to hold everything together. Of course, she wasn't frightened for herself. She did not matter. She saw herself as having become tainted by her dealings with the world; she was no longer a pure soul like May. All that mattered was that she fulfil her duty in caring for May, keeping her from all harm. Of course, to achieve this, Lizzie reasoned that she had to keep herself from harm too, but this was only so as to allow her to continue to care for May.

Desperate in the quiet darkness, searching for reassurance, Lizzie would sometimes pray, her prayers always an incongruous mix, concerned as they were with her adult fears but spoken in the naïve words and sing-song phrases of prayers learned long ago at Sunday school. Since those far off Sunday morning lessons, Lizzie had delved no deeper into her beliefs. Since Mother's death and with May's increasing frailty, Lizzie no longer felt the desire to go to church. God was simply another character in the community around her, albeit a distant and, for her, an uncommunicative one. He was real in the way that a cousin in far off Australia would be real. But, never having felt that it was her place to ask for or expect anything more, she had no mature, personal relationship with her God. The daunting church minister of her youth, bible brandished high for all to see, voice rattling the rafters, had instilled in Lizzie the grudgingly accepted duty and service of the prophets, but not the delight and joy of the psalms. The remote, unfathomable Being had taken Frank away, then Father and Mother. He had left Lizzie to cope with everything and care for May, alone. Where was His divine plan now?

On nights such as these, Lizzie would often weep quietly, regretting a lifetime's lost opportunities. And in crying herself to sleep, her worries for the future would remain unresolved for yet another night.

4

It was late afternoon and shadows were lengthening across the lawn.

Lizzie was pacing the verandah, scanning the darkening greenery of the garden. She should have been safely inside now, locking up, but May had been out, somewhere in the garden, for nearly an hour and was failing to answer as Lizzie called her to come back inside. May had never ignored her like this before and Lizzie was in a state of confusion. One moment she was sure that May was hiding from her, fully intending to stay out into the evening to defy her. But in the next moment, that certainty melted away. Perhaps May had fallen. Perhaps she'd even hit her head and was lying unconscious, unable to respond. Lizzie turned from anxiety to irritation and back again, over and over.

With every passing minute she grew increasingly agitated, pacing the verandah, back and forth and, as the darkness deepened further, she became increasingly conscious of the squeaking of the boards beneath her feet. The noise was so loud. How had she never noticed it before? She felt so exposed out here and imagined the noise drawing unseen eyes towards her, attracting the attention of terrible things hidden from her in the darkness. She wanted to run back to safety; to hide. But she couldn't run back inside; she had to find May.

Twice Lizzie walked to the top of the steps leading down to the garden and twice she backed away. There was at least some light here, filtering out to the verandah from the rooms inside, though Lizzie had, as usual, already pulled the blinds down. The weak light was not sufficient to allow her to see clearly, but it offered some slight comfort in the increasing gloom. Lizzie decided to stay here, near the light. She could wait a while longer. May would come back soon.

But time went by and May did not come back.

Barely managing to control the tone of her voice, Lizzie called out into the gathering dusk.

"May? Come back in now."

No response.

Now, all control gone, Lizzie's voice was sharp edged.

"For God's sake, May, come back in, right now!"

Still nothing.

For a third time Lizzie called out into the night but there was still no reply. She felt that the whole garden was holding its breath; blackness waiting for her to venture in. Blinking back frightened tears and breathing heavily, she took a step down from the verandah. As her shaking foot touched the wet grass, she stopped and listened. Nothing. She called to May again, whispering this time, a harsh, frightened rasp. But again, no reply.

Lizzie was familiar with the layout of the garden by daylight, but in darkness nothing was where it should be; everything was grotesque, larger, more barbed than she remembered. She paused. A slight breeze rustled the leaves on branches above her head and the twisted trunks of the old trees quietly creaked and groaned their resistance. Noises and sounds that would have passed unnoticed, part of the pleasant texture in the background of a sunny afternoon, were now eerily threatening; a hint of menace in the darkness.

Lizzie stepped down onto the lawn and began a few hesitant steps forward, water from the grass quickly soaking through her thin house slippers. She took another step. And another. And another. Eventually, she reached the far edge of the lawn.

That she had come this far without mishap should perhaps have reassured her. It did not. She had to struggle to control the shaking in her legs. Her breathing and her pounding heart were erratically hammering out unpredictable and frightening rhythms. She fought to hold back the rising wave of panic that threatened to overwhelm her.

To continue her search, she now had three options. To her left was the orchard, a small area, full of gnarled trees with twisted branches, which she really didn't want to go into tonight. To her right lay the wilderness area that May called her 'Wild Grove'. Ahead of her, was the small vegetable patch. That's where she'd be. Lizzie was sure. May would be in there.

She risked another urgent whisper,

"May. May, where are you? Please stop this nonsense. Where are you?"

Once her own voice had died away there was only the rustle of the leaves and the thumping of her heart. Clenching both fists so tightly that her nails dug into her palms, Lizzie drew one long, ragged breath, then moved towards the vegetable patch. She knew that May kept the plants here in good order. Everything would be in straight rows. Lizzie had only to find the path and she would be alright. Tentatively, she poked at the ground with her toe and miraculously came upon the gravel of the path immediately. She began slowly to edge forward, feeling ahead all the while with her toes, searching out the path. There was no sign of May. Lizzie felt around with her hands and was scratched by a briar for her trouble. If only there were a moon tonight, at least she would be able to see a little. Sucking her sore thumb, she again resorted to whispering.

"May? May, where are you? Are you in here? May, come on, please."

No reply.

Trying to make as little noise as possible, Lizzie walked the whole length of the pathway and bent low to the ground to see if May had fallen. But there was no sign, no indication of anything untoward. She turned and made her way back, to the edge of the lawn.

She now had the choice of the orchard or the Wild Grove. She steeled herself.

The orchard.

Walking in, Lizzie's feet soon became ensnared in the grass grown long and matted beneath the trees. She struggled forward and was bumped and scratched by the low branches, but she battled on until she thought she surely must have covered most of the area. In truth she couldn't really tell if she'd been going round in circles, but she had been searching a good twenty minutes before she gave up. Now she had to find her way back to the lawn and she had no idea in which direction it lay. Poor Lizzie was a further ten minutes stumbling around until, by chance, she came across the old gate post at the edge of the orchard. She was back at the lawn now. But still no sign of May. What could have happened to her?

This was a situation that Lizzie had dreaded all her adult life; something terrible had happened to May and Lizzie was unable to help her. Through so many dark, sleepless hours she had pictured May's panic; imagined her pitiful, lonely and afraid. But, now that the moment had come, had Lizzie been capable of such self-analysis, she would have had to admit that, initially, it was fear for her own safety that was uppermost in her mind, temporarily eclipsing the anxiety she felt for May. Lizzie had now been out of the house after dark for longer than at any time in the previous forty years. She was absolutely alone and surrounded by total darkness. Cold dread had seeped deep into her bones and, with stiffened limbs almost paralysed, Lizzie was terrified.

"I must get help," she gasped, "must get help."

She was debating with herself. Should she go for help rather than risk injury, or worse, in searching the Wild Grove? May grew all sorts of wild plants in there, in a random profusion, producing a tangle of intertwining stems and roots. In addition, many of May's cherished wild plants were armoured with thorns to catch the wary and there would be no straight gravel paths there.

It was to Lizzie's lasting credit that, despite her own terror, she now overcame her concerns for her personal safety. Grimly forcing herself to put thoughts of running for help out of her mind, she pushed her way into the enmeshed undergrowth of the Grove. Her face and hands were scratched and her normally tidy hair snagged by trailing brambles before she finally had to admit the impossibility of the search and ease herself back out to the lawn.

She stopped to catch her breath, her heart still thumping painfully. But, try as she might, she could not dispel the debilitating fear. There was no comfort whatsoever in the pitch darkness. It didn't offer concealment; rather, Lizzie sensed that, even now, the eyes of an attacker might be watching her, hidden from her sight by the same darkness that left her feeling exposed and vulnerable.

She had to get back to the house.

The weak light from the kitchen windows beckoned her. Holding her breath, she hurried across the lawn as quickly as possible, her feet slipping on the wet grass. Keeping low, she scrambled up the steps and fumbled frantically for the key.

"Hello."

Lizzie screamed and dropped the key. She fell to the floor feeling all around to find it. In absolute terror, she strained wide, tearful eyes trying to see into the inky darkness. Her end had come. She knew it.

The voice again, familiar now.

"Lizzie dear, is that you?"

May!

Instantly furious, Lizzie struggled to her feet. She couldn't see her sister yet, but her own face was blazing with emotion and her voice was equally fierce.

"May. What are you playing at? Where have you been?"

"I was in the garden and then I came to sit here, under the kitchen window."

"What!" Lizzie spat, "You've been here all this time and you let me search the whole garden for you, in the dark. How could you be so selfish? Look at me. I'm cut to ribbons." She moved towards the kitchen window, straining her eyes to see. "Where are you? Get inside now."

"No," came the simple reply.

Lizzie was shocked. For a moment she was speechless.

"You'll do as you're told, May. Get back in the house, now!"

"Not until you come and see this gorgeous moth, Lizzie. I think it might be a Polyphemus. They're not exactly rare, but I haven't seen one in our garden before. Do keep your voice down or you'll scare it off."

Lizzie simply could not believe what she was hearing. She marched over to the window and nearly fell headlong over May.

"Oh, you've frightened it."

Lizzie was incredulous.

"I've frightened **it**?" she spluttered, "I've frightened **it**? What about me? How could you let me be so worried about you and not call out to let me know you were safe? How could you?"

Oblivious to Lizzie's distress and saddened herself by the departure of the moth, May remained silent.

"Answer me, May! How could you treat me like that?"

When May still said nothing, Lizzie, exasperated, reached for her and dragged her to her feet. As she marched her towards the back door, Lizzie felt something underfoot. The key! She snatched it up and rattled it into the lock. Still holding May's arm in a painful grip, Lizzie opened the door and the two women all but fell inside. Releasing May, Lizzie quickly re-locked the door and sank, exhausted, into a chair.

May now tried to speak, but Lizzie raised a hand to silence her.

"Don't say another word. Just go. We'll talk about this tomorrow."

"But Lizzie."

"No. Not now."

Downcast, May walked from the room, the rubber tip of her walking stick squeaking on the tiled floor. Behind her, Lizzie sat staring into space. The terrible fear had subsided but she was still trembling and tears threatened to spill down her cheeks. Several minutes passed before she could gather herself, walk over and return the key to its hook by the back door.

Suddenly there was a knock at the front door.

Lizzie froze.

May hobbled back to the kitchen door.

"Lizzie, there's someone at the front door."

"Shhh!"

The knocking came again.

"Lizzie." May's eyes were pleading.

Suddenly re-energised, Lizzie walked over and took May by the arm. She pushed her firmly towards her bedroom.

"Go to your room and stay there. Quickly, go now!"

Lizzie watched as May slowly crossed the hall and closed the door of her room behind her. Then, swallowing hard, Lizzie crept towards the front door. The third knock was so loud that she literally jumped. She grabbed for something with which to steady herself and found she had clutched the back of a chair. She had to sit down. This was all too much. As she eased herself down, she looked up and saw the silhouette of a man through the window next to the door.

"Is anyone in there? This is the police. Is anyone in there?"

To her relief, the voice sounded friendly, reassuring; not threatening at all. Lizzie cleared her throat and answered.

"Yes I'm here", her voice trembled, "What do you want Officer?"

"Could I have your name please, Ma'am?"

She cleared her throat again.

"Elizabeth Atwell," then, as an afterthought, "Miss."

"Well, Miss Atwell, a couple parked down the street say they heard a scream from around here not long ago. I was driving by so they flagged me down to come check it out. Is everything OK ma'am?"

"Oh yes, everything is just fine, thank you."

"Did you hear any screams, Miss Atwell?"

Lizzie felt rather foolish and, for a moment, considered telling the officer that it had been May who shrieked. But those long ago Sunday school lessons had not all been in vain.

"It was me I'm afraid, Officer. My sister had gone out into the garden and when she didn't come back I was worried for her. I searched the garden for a long time and when I found her she gave me quite a start I can tell you. Usually I don't scare easily," she added, "I'm not that sort of person, but it was very dark by then."

"I understand. Now, Miss Atwell, could you do something for me? Could you open the door?"

"Why? Do I have to?"

"No, you don't have to, but I'd just like to assure myself that everything is OK before I leave. So, could you please open the door, Miss Atwell?"

Lizzie was uncertain. She liked the sound of his voice, but there was, of course, always the possibility that he wasn't really a police officer. She had no proof that he was. What if he was some criminal who was impersonating - yes, that was the word - impersonating a police officer. What should she do?

"I beg your pardon, Officer, but how do I know you are who you say you are?"

There was some movement beyond the door.

"Look. This is my ID, Miss Atwell. OK?"

The man was holding something against the glass of the window. Lizzie peered at it, unable to read any of the text through the frosted glazing. It occurred to her that, even had she been able to read it, she had no idea what a real police ID was supposed to look like.

"Please open the door Miss Atwell."

A floorboard squeaked at the end of the corridor. May had come out of her room.

"Are you there Lizzie? What are you going to do?" May whispered, her voice high with anxiety.

"I'm dealing with it." Lizzie hissed. "Go back into your room and stay there."

Lizzie had made her decision. She would open the front door.

She stood, pulled back the bolts and turned the key in the lock. Then she took a deep breath and pulled the door open as far as the chain would allow.

"Thank you Miss Atwell."

A torch light shone in her eyes.

"Please," she said, shielding her face with her hand, "the light."

With an apology the man turned off the torch. By the light from the hallway, he started to write something in a note pad. Free of the torch's glare, Lizzie began to make out some details of the young man's appearance. Most noticeable were his very pale grey eyes: such an unusual colour and set so wide apart. He was quite handsome she thought, surprising herself.

"Do you live here alone Miss Atwell?"

His question brought her back from her reverie.

"No, Officer, I live with my sister, May. We've lived in this house all our lives."

"Might I speak with your sister Miss Atwell?"

Lizzie hadn't expected that. Why did he want to speak to May? Surely that wasn't necessary.

"No. I'm afraid my sister has retired for the night."

He looked up from his note taking and fixed her with a keen stare as if trying to read something in her eyes. Lizzie smiled what she hoped was a reassuring smile. She didn't want May to have to come and speak to this man. He may have a fine face and a pleasant voice, but he was still a stranger and she had to protect her little sister from unknowns like him. The officer briefly looked down to check his notes, then seemed to make up his mind. He shut the book and pushed it back into his pocket.

"Well, we should let her sleep then. You're sure everything is OK?"

Lizzie nodded and he turned to leave. But just as she began to shut the door, the floorboard squeaked again. He stopped in mid stride and turned back towards her.

"What was that sound Miss Atwell? Could your sister have woken up, do you think?"

"No," Lizzie smiled that reassuring smile. "It's just these old houses, they creak and groan all the time."

He gave her that probing stare again and listened. Thankfully, no more noise came from the corridor.

"OK then. I'll be on my way. Good night Miss Atwell."

"Good night Officer. And thank you, it's so good to know that police are in the area. It makes me feel so much safer."

'If only that were true' she thought.

"It's all part of the service, Miss Atwell. Try not to worry, but in future perhaps you should do more of your gardening in daylight."

He smiled.

"Oh yes, Officer. I'm forever telling my sister to stay in after dark. I've told her it's not safe."

"Yeah, you might want to consider getting some outdoor lighting. You and your sister don't want to be having a fall."

"No. We certainly don't," Lizzie agreed, "Thank you Officer."

He smiled again.

"Well, if you're absolutely sure everything is OK, I'll say good night Miss Atwell."

"Yes. Goodnight Officer."

He nodded his farewell and turned to leave. As soon as he reached the top step, Lizzie shut the door quickly and pushed the bolts back into place. With a sigh, she sat down in the chair again.

"Lizzie?" A whisper came from the darkness of the

corridor. "Lizzie, are you alright?"

Hearing no reply May at once feared that something awful must have happened.

"Lizzie? Lizzie what's happening?"

Lizzie had heard her sister, but she felt in no hurry to respond. 'Let's see how May likes it when she calls out and no one answers her. Let's just see how she likes it.'

Both women were frozen, Lizzie sitting in the hall and May standing in the corridor. Neither made any sound. Minutes passed in this way until Lizzie became aware of an almost imperceptible sniffling. She rose and walked across the hall. May was standing, trembling slightly, in the middle of the corridor, eyes shut, tears streaming down her face. She was very frightened but had no idea what to do other than to stay absolutely still and silent and await whatever was to come.

Lizzie's resolve to punish May could not long withstand her sister's tears.

"I'm alright, you silly goose. Did you hear me May? I'm alright."

May came to life again, a huge smile of relief broke across her wet face. She wiped at her tears.

"Oh Lizzie, I was so worried."

"Well, now you have some idea of how I felt when I was outside looking for you."

May stopped, surprised.

"But Lizzie, that was completely different. I was just out looking for moths in our own garden. That's not the same as dealing with a stranger at the door in the middle of the night now is it?"

Lizzie couldn't believe it. May felt no remorse for all that she had put her through. Lizzie moved towards her sister and must have looked very angry because May backed away a step. Lizzie spoke grimly and with exaggerated slowness.

"He was a police officer May. And the only reason he came to our home was because someone heard us screaming. And we were only screaming like that because we were frightened, because we were out in the dark."

After a moment's pause, May said quietly, "I wasn't frightened Lizzie. I quite like the dark." again the hesitation, "And **I** didn't scream."

Lizzie was furious that May had seen her weak and afraid out in the garden, but she couldn't deny the truth behind what her sister was saying. Her own eyes were pricked with tears now: hot tears of frustration and exasperation.

"May," said Lizzie, controlling her voice only with great effort, "have you learnt nothing from this evening?"

"Like what, Lizzie?"

She was impossible!

"Like that I was right about being out in the dark. That it's dangerous. And the police officer agreed with me; he suggested we get security lights."

But May was not contrite. On the contrary she looked suddenly excited.

"Oh yes, lights would be marvellous for the moths. Can we do that?"

"Forget the damned moths will you? Can't you ever think of anything else?"

"I'm sorry Lizzie." May paused a moment, a show of contrition, then, "But can we get the lights?"

Lizzie gave up.

"No." she snapped, "We can't get security lights. We don't have the money."

May looked dismayed.

'Now,' thought Lizzie, 'now she looks sorry, but not because she broke her promise to Mother and worried me half to death, oh no. She's sad because she can't have some lights for her blessed moths.'

Lizzie was exhausted. It had been a horribly stressful evening and right now she was feeling her age. She couldn't cope with worries like this the way she used to. She needed rest.

"Go to bed, May. I'll lock up and then I'm for bed myself."

Long-faced, May turned away.

"Good night." she said without even looking back.

Behind her Lizzie leant back against the wall.

She could see her reflection in the hall mirror. Her hair was wild from her exertions in the garden. Her hands and face had several small scratches. What must the police officer have thought? No wonder he'd wanted reassurance that all was well. Lizzie let her shoulders sink. She was just too old and too tired. How she wished she could pass the responsibility for everything over to someone else.

But there was no one else.

Slowly, she raised herself. She walked through the ground floor rooms, checking the windows and closing all the doors behind her. At May's room she whispered a good night, but got no response. Last, she checked the kitchen. The windows were closed and securely locked. The stove was switched off. The back door was locked and the key hung there on its hook. Lizzie turned out the light and slowly went upstairs to bed.

In spite of her exhaustion Lizzie couldn't sleep. She turned the events of the evening over and over in her mind. In the dark of the early hours, the officer no longer seemed so plausible. Theirs was the only house at this end of the track so how likely was it that someone had heard her scream? And the officer had got to their house suspiciously quickly. How convenient that he had just happened by. And why had he wanted to know who lived here? Why did he need to know that? It was all very suspicious. The more she dwelt on their conversation, the more she regretted having answered as she had. When he asked her if she was alone, she should have lied. She should have invented a whole strapping family living here with her.

"Yes, I live here with my sons, my four grown sons." she whispered into the darkness of her bedroom, "They're all out at the moment but they'll be back any minute now."

No. That wouldn't have worked. He'd have wondered why a Miss Atwell had children. This was a small town, not the big city, after all.

"Your sons, Miss Atwell?" he'd have said, stressing the 'Miss'. He'd have known she was lying.

But no. Lizzie would have had an answer for that too.

"Yes Officer. Miss." she would have said, also stressing the 'Miss', "I'm divorced."

Pleased with this quick thinking, Lizzie smiled in the darkened room.

"Of course, of course. Thank you Miss Atwell." he would have said.

And he would have gone. It would have been that simple.

Why had she told him so much? Why had she told him about May being in the house?

When they heard the floorboard creak, she could have said it was her dog. A big dog. A German Shepherd.

A fierce dog and some burly sons would have been enough to make sure that the man left her alone if he were an impostor. And, if he had been a real police officer, what harm would there have been in a few white lies?

Oh, what had she done?

45

Weak light from the rising sun was already spilling into the room before Lizzie finally fell into welcome sleep.

5

Woken, after what seemed only minutes of sleep, by the sound of May's voice raised in a light-hearted song, Lizzie scowled. The night's passing had not lessened her anger at May's behaviour and it was too galling now to have to suffer such overt cheerfulness. Lizzie tried to pull the pillow over her ears, but it was no use, she could still hear quite well enough to be disturbed. Finally admitting defeat, she pulled herself upright and lowered her feet to the floor.

Getting her feet into her slippers was, as usual, a hit and miss affair; Lizzie's toes rarely homed into her slippers at the first attempt. Concentration was needed, over several attempts, till finally her toes slid home. It was only a small inconvenience, but it was the same performance every morning and it never failed to irritate her. Lizzie hated her body's failings. Being old was nothing but a nuisance. Nothing worked as it used to.

She sighed.

Downstairs May's singing rose to a joyful crescendo and Lizzie clapped her hands over her ears. How capricious the ageing process was; her joints stiffened, her skin sagged and her muscles wasted, so why did her hearing have to be so damn good? With an explosive grunt of effort, Lizzie raised herself up and angrily tugged her dressing-gown about her.

Lizzie found May busy in the kitchen. She looked up from her cooking with a smile. Unlike Lizzie, May had obviously slept very well indeed.

"Well, at last, Sleepy Head. I'd all but given you up."

Lizzie, after so little sleep, was in no mood for chatter.

"I didn't sleep well and I have a terrible headache." she answered flatly.

"Oh, I'm sorry, Lizzie dear. Was my singing too loud?"

"Yes."

May looked hurt for a moment but quickly recovered.

"Shall I make you some breakfast, dear?"

"No."

"No?"

"I'm not hungry."

Lizzie was not going to offer May any signs of politeness and certainly no smile. She spoke in a dull monotone and kept her face an unyielding blank. She wanted May to realise how much hurt she had caused by her selfishness last night. She wanted May to promise never to act like that again. She wanted an unreserved apology.

Once she had received such an apology Lizzie would then resume her accustomed role as the wise older sister whose acknowledged responsibility was to decide what was best for them both. Though the apology was deserved, and indeed overdue, Lizzie intended to accept it gracefully and forgive May with an injured, but understanding smile.

But Lizzie was in for a disappointment. No apology was forthcoming.

May had put the unpleasantness of the previous evening clear out of her mind. She was in contented mood and now set herself the task of sharing her good humour with her sister. She chattered on and on about the wonderfully sunny morning and the freshness of the air, all the while preparing her own breakfast. Every minute or so she rechecked with Lizzie that she was sure she didn't want anything to eat and each sullen answering shake of the head from Lizzie was met with a smiling shrug from May before she recommenced her chattering.

In the face of this onslaught of goodwill Lizzie could feel her own anger rising. Was this sister of hers going to pretend that last night hadn't happened? How could May treat her so badly? Lizzie's indignation demanded some recognition.

May had put one fried egg on her own plate and paused now, holding the frying pan angled over a second empty plate. She raised an enquiring eyebrow at Lizzie.

"Are you really sure, Lizzie dear? Last chance."

Lizzie could contain her irritation no longer.

"Don't you 'Lizzie dear' me. Don't you try to smother me with all this sugary sweetness and light. How can you act like this, as if last night hadn't happened?"

Confused, May didn't know what to say. She had no idea why Lizzie should be so angry. She remained frozen: utterly baffled. The second fried egg slid unheeded onto the table.

There was an awkward silence.

"Well?" Lizzie demanded.

May spoke quietly.

"Well what, dear? I don't understand."

She bit her lip nervously. This was obviously yet another one of those occasions where she had misunderstood what was happening. Lizzie must surely have some powerful grievance to be so very agitated, but May still wasn't sure what it might be.

"About last night, what have you got to say for yourself?" Lizzie demanded, exasperated.

Again there was a pause as May struggled for words. Lizzie waited.

At last May tried,

"I'm very sorry you were upset last night, Lizzie. I hope you feel better now."

It was a hope not likely to be realised.

"You hope I'm feeling better? Is that the best you can do? I was only upset last night because of you. Because you broke your promise to Mother, and to me, by wandering off in the dark."

"I didn't wander off Lizzie. I just went for a walk in our own garden. And, after that, I just sat on the verandah." May inclined her head towards the window.

"After dark," said Lizzie, "you were out after dark. And anything could have happened. You could have fallen, or been hurt or anything."

"But nothing did happen Lizzie. You didn't need to be worried at all."

"So you did realise that I was worried? You realised and yet you went out anyway? Well, thank you very much."

"Lizzie, it's not like that. It's just that you always worry too much."

"What?"

"You do. You worry about everyone and everything. You always have. You should learn to trust people a bit more and then you wouldn't be so anxious all the time. You know, I sometimes think that you make things much harder for yourself than they need be."

"I make things harder do I?" asked Lizzie, her questioning voice deceptively calm.

May completely misread Lizzie's measured tone and mistakenly believed that she was winning her sister over.

"Yes dear," she said, her voice encouraging, "I'm sure things aren't as bad as you imagine."

"So it's only in my imagination that I have to look after you and keep both of us safe is it?"

"No, dear I -"

"It's all in my head is it?"

"No. I'm not saying that. It's just that I think you expect the worst all the time and life isn't all bad is it? I mean, we're lucky aren't we? Our life is a good one. We live in a nice house, in a pleasant neighbourhood of good, ordinary folks."

"And how do you know that? How do you know anything about what's going on in the world out there?"

"Lizzie, I'm sorry-"

"Forget it! It's too late to say sorry now. I don't know why I waste my time."

Lizzie walked briskly to the door, then, without turning, added, "You'd better clear that up before it stains the cloth."

May looked down, noticing the fallen egg for the first time. How had that happened? She sighed.

She would tidy the mess directly after breakfast.

Lizzie spent the rest of the morning dusting the books that crammed the shelves covering two walls of what had once been their father's study. He'd called it his den, his secret hideout, when Lizzie was a child, before he went off to the war. In those carefree early days there had been a big comfortable chair by the fire and humorous cartoons from the newspapers framed on the wall. On the mantle there used to be a very battered and faded top hat that Father had used in performing simple magic tricks and next to the hat, she remembered, there had been a small card, hand-painted for him by Frank, which read, 'Bee Earnest', the words written in a child's wobbly hand. The card also had a rather poorly drawn picture of a bee.

Her father had loved this childish play on his name.

His own boyhood friends and schoolmates had first called him Ernest B. (The 'B' was for Benedict; Ernest Benedict Atwell). They had soon modified this to 'Ernest the Bee' and the nickname had stayed with him into adulthood. Father had originally given Frank's work of art pride of place over the fireplace. But after his return from the war Father had taken to calling the room his study. From then on it was an altogether more serious place and, at some point, Lizzie couldn't remember when, the cartoons, the top hat and the Bee Earnest card had been taken down and never replaced.

Absently dusting, Lizzie's mind had turned, of course, to memories of Frank, but also to wondering what dreadful things must have happened in the war to have effected such a great change in their father. She had often wondered what sights he must have seen and what horrors he must have witnessed, but he had never spoken of his wartime experiences, certainly not to the children and, Lizzie suspected, probably not even to their mother. Keeping all the traumatic images to himself had not, Lizzie thought, been the best way for him to deal with them. It was too late now, of course, but even all these years after his death, Lizzie still felt great regret at the loss of the carefree father she had known, all too briefly, as a child.

Lizzie shook her dusting cloth out of the window and then re-locked the window carefully before surveying the room. She was pleased with the result of her morning's labour. The room looked cared for. Satisfied that she had earned a cup of coffee, she crossed the hallway to the kitchen.

"Oh, for goodness sake, May." she muttered.

May was not there, but Lizzie had noticed, with some disgust, that May had not cleaned away the egg. It now lay congealed on the tablecloth, a slick halo of fat darkening the material around it. Moving the small vase of flowers aside, Lizzie folded the cloth over. She shook the egg loose and threw it away. Was that so difficult? Why couldn't May have done it? Why did Lizzie always have to do everything? As she waited for the sink to fill, Lizzie angrily prodded the cloth under the bubbling water. She was muttering to herself, bemoaning May's irritating lack of organisation, when, looking up, she glanced out of the window. Abruptly, her words stopped dead. Lizzie froze.

There was a man in the garden.

Lizzie had caught a fleeting glimpse of him as he slipped into the orchard. Seconds later, everything in the part of the garden visible from the window looked completely normal again. Nothing was out of place or apparently disturbed. Backing away from the window, Lizzie looked to check that the door to the verandah was locked.

It was not.

She quickly turned the key. Her heart began to quicken but she controlled her breathing in an effort to calm herself. She must find May. She would be inside the house as she never did her gardening until the afternoon, so Lizzie went to the hall and called to May in as loud a whisper as she dared use. No reply. Straining to hear any tiny response, Lizzie was suddenly startled by a sound at the back door.

She edged back into the kitchen and, as quietly as possible, slid a knife out of the drawer. She took a deep breath and approached the back door. The tapping sound came again and, this time, a familiar voice.

"Lizzie? Lizzie, would you please unlock the door?" It was May and she sounded confused, "Lizzie? What's going on?"

Lizzie quickly went to unlock the door. She opened it

and pulled May in before she could say another word, re-locking the door immediately.

May was shaken.

"Whatever's the matter Lizzie? Why did you lock me out? You're not still cross from this morning are you?"

"Shh! There's a man in the garden."

Immediately silenced, May joined Lizzie peering through the window.

"Where?"

"He's gone into the orchard."

May went pale.

"But I was just in the orchard. Oh my goodness."

May sat down rather quickly. There was a roaring in her ears and she began to feel light-headed. Lizzie could see that her sister was close to fainting.

"Stay calm May. The doors are all locked and I have this."

Lizzie opened her hand to reveal the knife. May was shocked. Her hand went to her chest and she swallowed hard.

"Heavens, Lizzie, what are you thinking? Put that down, please. You're going to get yourself hurt."

Realising that she must look rather foolish, a wiry old lady brandishing a paring knife, Lizzie lowered the blade.

"You wait here May."

"Why?" May gasped, "What are you going to do?"

"I'll go up to the landing window to have a look down on the garden."

"Please don't be long, Lizzie."

Lizzie climbed the stairs and peered out of the large window at the end of the landing corridor. The window gave out onto the low roof of the utility room, and beyond that it gave a good view over most of the garden. Lizzie could see nothing out of the ordinary so she went back down to May.

"He must have gone."

May relaxed at once. She said nothing, but Lizzie could tell what that silence meant.

"There really was a man there, May," she insisted.

Still May said nothing.

"You don't believe me?" Lizzie was indignant.

May raised her eyebrows.

"Well he's not there now is he, dear?"

May left the room without another word and Lizzie could do no more than watch her go. She tried to reassure herself. She had seen a man. She had. She was sure of it. At length she realised that the paring knife was still in her hand. She released it and let it fall, clattering, into the sink.

Despite Lizzie's best efforts to suppress them, doubts began to form so that, by the time she and May were sitting down for their supper that evening, Lizzie was quite willing to believe that she had been day dreaming. She now supposed that it could have been a trick of the light, or perhaps an animal. Certainly she was no longer completely convinced it had been a man. May for her part was almost certain that Lizzie had invented this intruder in order to scare her, but she didn't resent the invention because she knew that Lizzie always acted with the best of intentions. Lizzie would only have concocted this story because she was worried for May's safety; she wanted May to stay indoors, away from harm. But why had Lizzie pretended that she'd seen someone in the garden in broad daylight, when she had never before raised any objection to May going out during the day? That was strange. Surely Lizzie just wanted to stop her going out at night. May shrugged. She couldn't make sense of it. But she was quite used to misunderstanding the motivations of others, so she put that concern out of her mind.

They ate their meal in a silence broken only by the cold scraping of cutlery, the noisy ingestion of soup through sparse teeth and the gentle tearing of the home baked bread, to mop the bowls clean of every last drop. It was only at the end of the meal that May finally spoke.

"Lizzie, I'm going to go out and watch the moths again this evening."

She was risking angering Lizzie and normally she wouldn't dream of crossing her, but this really was such a little thing. Surely Lizzie would come round to her view soon.

Lizzie was, as expected, dismayed at May's announcement, but, less predictably, she said nothing in response to it. On any other occasion, she would have argued her case strongly and invoked May's promise to their mother. Ordinarily, she would have forced May to do as she was told, for her own good, of course. But Lizzie was not herself. After making such a fuss this afternoon, over a man that she now doubted having seen, she was dispirited and preoccupied. She was experiencing what was, for her, an unusual lack of self-confidence. It was May's good fortune that, her mind elsewhere, Lizzie felt unable to participate in a conversation.

"I'm hoping to see that Polyphemus again Lizzie." May continued, hardly daring to believe how well this was going, "It's very pretty. Perhaps you'd join me? I'm only going to sit out on the verandah. We needn't go far away from the lights of the house."

May hadn't dared hope for easy acceptance and was quietly amazed when Lizzie distractedly muttered,

"Oh I don't know. Maybe." Lizzie slowly drew herself up, "I'm sorry May, but I must go and sit down for a little while. Do you mind clearing the dishes?"

"Of course not, Lizzie." May was delighted and full of

sisterly concern. "You go and have a little rest. I'll bring you a cup of camomile tea later."

Sitting out on the verandah several hours later, May was not surprised that Lizzie had after all chosen to stay inside rather than join her out here. It was a cold evening. May was warmly dressed and had a rug tucked over her legs but, little by little, the chill air seeped in, fingering a path through the folds of material to settle its icy touch on her. The cold in her limbs was further exacerbated by the need to sit as still as possible so as to avoid disturbing the insects. Eventually, her patience was rewarded: the Polyphemus landed on the other chair. May could see it plainly. It was enormous; its wingspan easily eight inches. Its top wings were a reddish-brown and, as if to reward May for her devotion, the moth was clearly displaying the huge eyes on its under wings. May was delighted.

"Thank you." she breathed.

May was startled to hear a voice.

"For what?"

Lizzie had come out after all.

"Oh, Lizzie, it's gone now but did you see it? It was the Polyphemus: the one I saw yesterday."

"I didn't see anything. Do you know what time it is? You shouldn't have let me sleep so long." Lizzie's voice was still lacking her usual energy, "Come in now for pete' sake."

May was so pleased to have seen the moth again that she made no attempt to argue. She gathered up her rug and followed Lizzie into the house.

6

That night, to her relief, Lizzie slept well, untroubled by fears or bad dreams. She came down to the kitchen in the morning feeling quite her old self. Unlike May, Lizzie couldn't simply consign unsettling memories to some rarely visited corner of her mind, but she was able to rationalise. Clearly she had been very tired yesterday, overtired in fact, and she had probably just mistaken a fleeting shadow for an intruder. She'd been feeling the strain of responsibility increasingly difficult to bear lately and stress, coupled with tiredness, could cause anyone to make a mistake like that.

It was her turn to make breakfast and she was already stirring the tea in the large china pot when May appeared. Lizzie was back in charge. She pointed May to a chair.

"Sit down May and have some toast."

"I will, thank you." May eased herself into a chair, resting her stick against the table. She took a piece of toast and began to spread it with butter. "Are you feeling better Lizzie?" she asked, without looking up from her task.

Lizzie's answer was brisk.

"Absolutely fine. Why shouldn't I be?"

"Oh, no reason, dear."

Lizzie poured the tea and they settled to eating their

breakfast with little further conversation. When they had finished, May watched Lizzie take the empty plates to the sink. May smiled and got to her feet, but before carrying her own tea cup to the sink, she said.

"It means a lot to me that you were able to join me last evening Lizzie. I was so pleased."

"Well, don't be," said Lizzie sourly, "I only came out to get you to come back in."

May smiled again. Lizzie didn't like overt shows of affection or concern; they made her uncomfortable.

"Will you come out this evening Lizzie? Oh please, will you?"

In the silence that followed, Lizzie tried to decide how best to tell May that neither of them would be going out after dark ever again. Maybe there hadn't really been a man in the garden yesterday, but there was real crime in the world and wicked people who would make short work of her naïve and trusting sister.

"No, I won't." she said, "And neither will you."

May was taken aback.

"Oh, come now, Lizzie, we're not going to argue about this again are we?"

"No. We're not. You must simply promise me that you won't go out like that again. Ever. And this time, May, you must mean it."

May sounded confused.

"But you came out last evening."

"I wasn't myself yesterday and you took advantage of that to sneak out while I was resting. That was a very foolish and a very dangerous thing to do."

"I didn't 'sneak out' I simply slipped out quietly so as not to wake you."

Lizzie was clearly unimpressed.

"I don't care how you describe your behaviour. What you did was foolish. As I've told you, so many times, it's a very dangerous world out there and we must take sensible steps to keep ourselves safe. Thank goodness, I'm thinking clearly again this morning. And you must listen to me; it's not safe to go wandering about in the garden after dark. You mustn't do it again."

"But this isn't fair, Lizzie. You know how much I enjoy watching the moths. It's my greatest love. Please let's not fight over this."

"Don't be ridiculous. We won't fight, but you must see the sense in what I'm telling you and you must do as I say."

Before May could say anything more, Lizzie picked up her handbag. With a cursory glance, she checked that her purse was inside and, satisfied, she snapped it shut. Already walking to the door, she picked up May's library book from the dresser.

"I must go into town now. Think over what I've said. We'll speak again when I get back."

Lizzie walked briskly down the hall to the front door. Behind her, May stood framed in the kitchen doorway, her mouth open and a look of petulant disbelief on her face.

"This isn't fair Lizzie!" she almost shouted.

"We'll talk when I get back."

Lizzie looked May in the eye, then pulled the front door closed.

It was a Monday, so Lizzie walked to the library building, to exchange May's loaned book and read the newspapers. Miss Willets, the librarian, smiled in recognition as Lizzie entered. Lizzie nodded in response and handed her May's old book, accepting a new one selected by Miss Willets without even bothering to read its title. Lizzie then took her accustomed seat by the window. The newspapers were displayed on the stand to her left and she helped herself to several of them, spreading them open on the wide table. She took out her reading glasses and settled herself.

The front pages made grim reading. The headlines detailed a series of murders. Four young men, all suspected gang members, had died in a gunfight. It had something to do with drugs. Lizzie made a tutting sound with her teeth. It was so often to do with drugs. People would do anything to get their fix. She smiled a humourless smile as it occurred to her that May was so out of touch with events that she wouldn't even know what a 'fix' was. How could she think she knew about the world? Lizzie shook her head and read on. The robberies, muggings and killings, the meat of most front pages, all served yet again to reinforce her conviction that the world she and May had once known was gone forever. All she could do was to hold on to the last remnants of their former life and try to keep the modern world and its wickedness at bay.

For an hour or so, Lizzie read on, devouring every detail, no matter how unsettling the subject matter. When she had finished, she neatly refolded the papers and returned them to the stand, nodded a farewell to Miss Willets and left the building, feeling dismayed yet also oddly reassured.

After an uneventful walk home, Lizzie performed her usual speedy unlocking of the front door. Stepping inside, she gasped to find May standing right there, behind the door, waiting for her.

"Lizzie. You really can't stop me going out in my own garden. It's ridiculous."

From just a glance at her face it was clear to Lizzie that May was very angry, but Lizzie's determination was equal to May's sense of injustice and she recovered quickly from her initial surprise.

"Have you been standing there since I left?" she asked, not expecting a reply, "Well, you might at least let me get the shopping put away before you start arguing with me."

May followed her into the kitchen in silence and stood as Lizzie heaved the bag up onto the table.

"Well?" May said at last.

"Make yourself useful and put these pickles away."

For a second May refused to take the proffered jar, her face an elderly mimic of a sullen adolescent, then she snatched the jar from Lizzie's hand.

"Careful," muttered Lizzie, fully conscious of the irritation she was causing her sister.

They put away the remaining items in stony silence.

"Can we talk now?" asked May once they had finished.

"There's not really much to talk about is there? It's not safe to be out after dark and that's all there is to it."

"I beg your pardon?" said May indignantly, "Why should you decide what's safe for me and what's not?"

Lizzie was shocked.

"Why should I? Why? Because I have to make all the important decisions around here, that's why. Because I have to do all the shopping and run all the errands, pay all the bills and deal with all the tradesmen, plumbers and electricians. Because you chose not to involve yourself in any of that and I have to do all of it. I know what the world is like and you have no idea. That's why I decide what's safe for both of us. Because I know and you don't."

May was stunned by this outburst. She struggled for a response.

"That's not fair." she said at last, "You know I can't walk very well with my arthritis. I couldn't run errands and do the shopping. You know that."

"Let's not fool ourselves, May. You never ran errands or did anything remotely practical even before you had

63

arthritis. Well, did you?"

Again May searched for words.

"I grow the flowers, the vegetables and the barley. I make all the bread. I tend the trees in the orchard and collect the fruit. That's all practical, isn't it? And I could have done those other things you said too, when I was younger, but you always wanted to be in charge. You always had to be in control and you wouldn't have let me."

"Oh please! When did you ever ask to do any of it? Never. Not once. No, you've always been quite happy to sit back and let me do everything."

May's eyes, always watery, were now stinging. Soon the tears would flow and she wouldn't be able to stop them. Lizzie had never spoken to her like this. Never. May felt bruised. How could Lizzie resent her so much? Lizzie was presenting everything as simple black and white, right and wrong, but it wasn't like that. She worked every bit as hard as Lizzie, or at least as hard as she was able. It simply wasn't fair.

After a prolonged silence, May lifted her head defiantly.

"Lizzie," she said in a quiet voice, "can you honestly say that you would have let me do any of those things if I had asked? Just you think about that, Miss 'I'm your older sister so you must do as I say'."

Lizzie didn't have a quick answer, but she didn't need one. May was already hobbling out of the kitchen. Behind her, Lizzie braced herself for the noise of the shutting door, expecting May to slam it, but she did not. May masked her struggle to hold back her tears with a show of quiet dignity. She went to her own room and gently shut the door behind her.

To Lizzie, left standing at the kitchen table, the victory, if victory it was, seemed hollow. May's last question was the difficult one. Deep down inside, Lizzie recognised that May was actually right; Lizzie didn't want her to take over any of the dealings with outsiders. She didn't want May to become tainted by any contact with the outside. It was bad enough that one of them had to go out and about in the world, but it couldn't be May.

Lizzie now felt rather ashamed for the arguments that she had used, but she soon put a stop to that line of thought. The end had justified the means. She had to do whatever was necessary to keep May safe. She had promised. Her duty was to protect May, even from herself.

May stayed in her room for the rest of the afternoon and eventually Lizzie decided to make May's favourite teacakes in order to tempt her to come out. She opened the kitchen door to let the sweet smell of baking permeate the house. Then she prepared a fresh pot of tea before calling May.

May ignored her call at first but, after a few minutes, Lizzie heard her footsteps and the soft squeak of her stick on the kitchen tiles. She decided to let May be the first to speak and quietly busied herself laying the table. But May said nothing. She simply stood in the kitchen doorway and stared at her, in silence. Lizzie was irritated by this sullen behaviour but she bit her lip and tried to be patient. May would speak when she was ready. It's no easy thing to admit that you are wrong.

Lizzie went to fetch the jam from the larder and, when she returned, found that May was finally willing to talk.

"I've seen it again Lizzie."

Lizzie hadn't expected this as an opener.

"I've seen it again," May insisted, "just now. Here in the house."

"Seen what?"

"The Polyphemus, the moth, like the one I saw yesterday and the day before, but this one was even bigger, even more magnificent. Have you seen it?"

"No I haven't." Lizzie was annoyed but tried to stay calm, "But I hardly think that a moth is very important right now, do you?

May said nothing and Lizzie continued, in the same measured tones.

"Have you given any thought to what I said this morning? Do you understand now that you mustn't go out after dark?"

No response.

"Well?"

"I'm not hungry. I feel nauseous," said May all at once, "I'm going back to my room."

"Oh, for pete's sake May," Lizzie called after her, "don't be so childish."

"Why not?" May snapped, "You treat me like a child."

She shouted an angry, "Good night," before slamming her bedroom door.

For a moment Lizzie waited to see if May would reappear but, as she did not, Lizzie ate her supper alone and then cleared the dishes away. She put the leftover teacakes into a cake tin in the larder; May would be hungry in the morning.

This evening Lizzie decided not to sit for a while after her meal as she usually did. It wouldn't do to fall asleep in her armchair as she had yesterday. She went from room to room, performing her usual ritual of closing and locking, finishing, as always, back in the kitchen. She hung the key on its hook and turned off the water dripping into the sink. From the hall door she did her last check of the kitchen, switched off the light and shut the door, before gratefully climbing the stairs to her bedroom.

7

It seemed to Lizzie that she had only just begun to slip towards deep sleep, when she was woken by a noise. It had been loud enough to wake her, but too brief for her to identify. She sat up in bed, the movement making the bedsprings scrape and squeak. She had to sit absolutely still, allowing the squealing oscillations to subside, before she could hear anything else. When the springs finally lapsed into silence, she held her breath and listened hard.

Nothing.

What on earth could it have been? A floorboard flexing as it slowly cooled? No, Lizzie was too well used to the sounds of this old house to be woken by a squeaking floorboard. Perhaps it had been a mouse scrabbling about up in the loft. But no, she decided it was most likely May finally getting herself something for supper. It was just surprising that there wasn't any further sound from the kitchen, which was directly below Lizzie's room. She sighed. It had probably been no more than May clumsily refitting the lid on the cake tin, but now Lizzie wouldn't be able to get back to sleep until she knew for sure. There was nothing for it but to investigate.

Scowling, irritated at the renewed grating of the springs, Lizzie swung her feet over the edge of the bed. Again, there was the tiresome difficulty in guiding feet into slippers. Lizzie then pulled on her dressing gown and, pausing only briefly to pat her hair into a semblance of order, went down to the hall. She fully expected to find May sitting at the kitchen table, chewing a teacake in careful silence, the light intentionally left off so as to avoid attracting Lizzie's attention. But, as Lizzie switched the flickering strip into life, the harsh light showed there to be no one in the kitchen. Disconcerted, she went to the larder and found the teacakes all there in the cake tin, just as she had left them.

With a sudden chill, it struck her: if May had not made the sound, then who had? Lizzie suddenly felt very vulnerable, here in the middle of her own kitchen. She had come down from her room carelessly, as she would on any morning, not even making an effort to avoid the two noisy treads on the stairs. Had she inadvertently alerted an intruder to her presence? Was someone, even now, watching her from the shadows in the hallway? Her legs begin to shake. She steadied herself, struggling to keep her mind from running headlong into panic. She scanned the room, her searching eyes quickly coming to rest on the backdoor. The key was in the lock though Lizzie knew she had left the key on its hook as she always did: it was part of her routine as it had been for years. She took a deep, steadying breath then, as quietly as possible, crossed the kitchen to the door. She tried to turn the doorknob. The door remained closed. So it was still locked, that was something. Unconsciously, she removed the key from the lock and put it back on its hook. She was now thinking fast. Whoever had locked the door must still be inside the house. She discounted the possibility that May had gone out. It was bad enough that she sometimes stayed out late into the evening, but that was very different from going out alone after darkness had already fallen, while Lizzie was asleep.

Lizzie had to do something. She had to act. But her feverish casting about, trying to decide what to do, drew a blank; she'd never anticipated this situation; she had no plan. Besides her own personal fear, only one thought dominated; she must get to May. She must assure herself that May was safe.

Lizzie took a knife from the drawer, as she had before. It reassured her, although she felt quite faint at the prospect of actually using it to harm anyone, even an intruder. She stood next to the hall doorway, gripped the knife in her right hand and put her left arm around the door frame, feeling for the light switch in the hall. She switched the light on and held her breath, expecting something to happen.

Nothing did.

Slowly, swallowing hard, Lizzie peeped out into the hall. The room seemed empty and there was no sign of any disturbance, but Lizzie felt no sense of relief; this was merely a temporary respite, a postponement of the inevitable confrontation. She eased herself out of the kitchen and crept along the corridor, towards May's bedroom.

Lizzie's hand went up automatically to knock on May's door, but she came to her senses and stopped herself just in time. She took a deep breath and, half-dreading what she might find, turned the handle to open the door. As her eyes became accustomed to the gloom, she could make out May's prone form in the bed. Lizzie listened but couldn't hear breathing. She leaned forward to listen more closely, steadying herself on the back of May's bedside chair. As her hand closed on the material on the chair, she stopped; the material was damp and cold, very cold. But, how could that be? The room was warm. Confused, Lizzie stepped to one side and let light from the corridor flood past her into the room. Now illuminated, thrown carelessly over the back of the chair, was the rug that May used when she sat out in the garden.

May had been out!

She had crept out in the middle of the night and sneaked back in again, leaving the key in the door. And she was lying there now, possibly pretending to be deep in sleep.

Lizzie's first instinct was to wake May and shout at her until all her anger was spent, but she stayed her hand as a better plan flashed into her mind. She tiptoed her retreat from the room and shut the door with such care that the catch merely whispered into place. Hurrying back to the kitchen, she went straight to the back door. She fingered the key on its hook, a moment of indecision. It would be better if she took care of the key, wouldn't it? May couldn't then be tempted to go out late ever again.

Lizzie made her decision. Yes, it was for May's safety, so it must be right. She took the key off its hook and went over to the dresser. Rummaging around in the top drawer, she came across what she was looking for and pulled out a length of red ribbon. Frowning with concentration, she threaded the key onto the ribbon, tied it and then, with some difficulty, put the ribbon around her neck. The key was cold against her skin but she patted it beneath her night-dress and smiled. It was for May's own good. It was the right thing to do.

Early the following morning, after a good night's sleep, May dressed and prepared for her day, cheerfully unsuspecting, brimming with pride in her achievement. If Lizzie would insist on thinking she knew best, then nocturnal excursions would simply have to be a secret kept from her. May was amazed at how easy it had been to slip out after dark. For two nights now she had spent a wonderful couple of hours watching her beloved moths and had returned feeling tired but also exhilarated by her daring. Admittedly, she had been rather concerned by the shutting click of the backdoor last night, it had sounded horribly loud in the otherwise silent house. Tonight she would be more careful and ease the door shut more slowly. It wouldn't be a problem.

After such an exciting evening, May had experienced no difficulty in sleeping, nodding off as soon as her head touched the pillow, to enjoy a wonderfully deep sleep. Making her way to the kitchen this morning, May felt she had a spring in her, usually shuffling, step. She was happy.

Her contentment was to be short lived.

When she took the kettle to the sink, she passed the backdoor and realised, without even having been aware she was looking for it, that the key was not on its hook. Putting down the kettle, she dabbed at her weepy eyes, blinked hard and stared again at the hook. No key. Suddenly confused, May abandoned the breakfast preparations and started to hunt for the key. She had to find it before Lizzie came down. It had to be here, somewhere. She searched the table, the floor and every other flat surface in the kitchen with no success. She used her stick to sweep back and forth under the cupboards but found nothing save spiralling ribbons of dust and fluff.

May went back down the corridor to her own room. Taking up the rug, she shook it as vigorously as she could, but no key fell to the floor. She undid and remade her bed, a huge exertion, searched her bedside table and chair and even felt through yesterday's dirty laundry, all to no avail. She had lost the key. What on earth was she going to tell Lizzie? May was so unnerved at the prospect that she had to sit down, her heart racing.

And there she remained for some time, the breakfast

forgotten, coming to life again only when she heard Lizzie's footsteps on the landing overhead. May got to her feet as quickly as possible, grunting at the complaints of her reluctant joints. She hurried to the door and called up to Lizzie.

"Lizzie? How would you like to breakfast in style this morning?"

Lizzie appeared at the bottom of the stairs and looked quizzically at her sister.

"Whatever do you mean?"

"I just thought it might make a pleasant change to have breakfast in the parlour today, rather than in the kitchen. What do you say?"

"Fine by me," answered Lizzie, "but won't that mean extra work for you, carrying things through from the kitchen?"

"Oh, I don't mind. If you come to the kitchen door, I'll pass the tea and toast to you and you can put them on the table for me."

When Lizzie made as if to follow her to the kitchen, May stopped, blocking her path,

"It's not ready yet. You go and sit down. I'll call you when it's ready."

May went on into the kitchen and hastily started making the breakfast. Lizzie took her seat in the parlour, smiling in spite of herself. Of course May wouldn't want her to go into the kitchen: she would notice that the key was missing. Lizzie's smile was one of both satisfaction and pity. Perhaps she should just tell May that the key was not lost but quite safe, hanging from a ribbon around her neck. That would be the kindest course of action, but Lizzie was not feeling generous towards her sister. Her smile hardened. It might do May some good to suffer a little. She had after all caused Lizzie a great deal of unnecessary worry lately. Yes, May deserved to be taught a lesson. Lizzie resolved to say nothing.

"Lizzie? The toast is ready."

Lizzie could hear the strain in her sister's voice as she strove to sound bright and untroubled. Lizzie's smile came back and there was little pity in it now.

"Coming." she answered sweetly.

Lizzie took a moment to compose a look of concern on her face, then went to the kitchen door.

"Oh May, you shouldn't be trying to carry the tray this far." she said, "Think of your arthritis. Let me come in and get the tea."

May's eyes were saucers of alarm.

"No. I'm fine, really. Take this, then go sit down."

Lizzie shrugged and let her eyes search, apparently for reassurance, in May's.

"Are you sure, dear?"

"Yes, really," May insisted, handing Lizzie the toast, "now, you go sit down."

As she turned away Lizzie couldn't prevent her amusement showing on her face. Poor May. She almost felt sorry for her.

Lizzie started to butter the toast while she waited for May to return. She held down the slice, steering the small lump of butter around with the knife. Gradually, without realising what she was doing, she slowed her hand to a stop. She stared at the toast, fascinated, watching the butter melt and run a golden path across the pitted surface. She was amazed that she'd never before taken the time to really look, to see how the rolling liquid gold magically disappeared into the pores on the surface of the toast, vanishing clean away. One moment it was there, the next, it was gone. Amazing!

Suddenly becoming aware that she was acting strangely, Lizzie blinked and pulled herself upright. What silliness! What was so fascinating in melting butter? She shook herself, put down the toast and tried to gather her thoughts. After a moment's confusion, her face once again broke into a smile: she had remembered why it was that she was eating here in the parlour. Her smile broadened in anticipation: she could now settle back and enjoy poor May's discomfort.

May struggled into the room carrying the tea pot.

"Let me pour, May. You look exhausted." Lizzie said, her solicitous tone matched by the look on her face, a picture of sisterly concern.

May's face was all gratitude.

"Oh. I'm fine, but, yes, thank you."

Lizzie should have been ashamed of her behaviour, but to her amazement she was feeling no guilt whatsoever, simply the enjoyment of power. She was playing with May as would a cat with a fallen bird. They ate their breakfast, Lizzie smiling and making small talk, but all the while observing the situation with detachment, savouring the thrill of possessing secret knowledge: being in total control. Without realising it, she had made the decision to leave telling May about the key for a good, long, time.

This was proving to be unexpectedly entertaining.

Naturally Lizzie was unsurprised at May's insistence that she would tidy the dishes away herself, but she protested half-heartedly, maintaining her pretense of concern.

"Really May," she said, "you should let me help."

Then, with unaccustomed malice, she decided to turn up the heat.

"May," she asked, "why are you being so very kind to me today?"

May avoided her gaze, apparently concentrating instead on sweeping from the table cloth into her palm the seeds and grains fallen from the toast.

"I...I just thought you deserved a treat because, as you

said yourself, you do such a lot for me. I just wanted to say thank you."

"I thought perhaps it was because you've reconsidered the other things I was saying yesterday."

May said nothing.

"You remember," Lizzie coaxed, "about not going out after dark?"

Puzzled, May finally looked up and met her sister's sympathetic gaze, straining to see what lay behind that solicitous look. Did Lizzie know she'd gone out last night? Did she somehow know that the key was missing or had she perhaps heard that noisy back door? May searched her sister's concerned expression. But Lizzie was giving nothing away.

"Perhaps we could talk about this later, Lizzie. I'd like to make a start on these dishes now."

So saying, May gathered up the plates and hobbled out of the room, leaving Lizzie feeling slightly flat. She had been enjoying this game of cat and mouse and hadn't wanted it cut short. Also, in leaving the room without answering her question, May had wrested back some control of the situation and Lizzie was not willing to let go her dominance. She left the table and walked towards the kitchen. May met her in the hall and shooed her back into the parlour, fussing like a mother hen.

"Can't you sit still for one minute? You're supposed to be letting me clear up."

Lizzie felt a surge of petulance at being herded in this manner.

She hit back.

"Any one would think you're trying to keep me out of the kitchen."

There was an instant's hesitation, a nervous lowering of the eyes, before May said, "Don't be silly, dear."

May attempted a thin smile as she dried her hands on

her apron, the activity a nervous distraction.

Lizzie inclined her head.

"You can tell me, May." she prompted, "Have you broken something?"

"No, of course not."

Lizzie managed to resist the urge to add, 'Or lost something perhaps?' That would have given the game away, and she wanted this game to last a while longer.

Leaving May to clear the breakfast away, Lizzie again spent several hours in her father's study. Looking through old photographs, she was soon so absorbed in the images of the past that she became oblivious to the poorly stifled noises arising from May's continuing search for the key. Lost in her memories, Lizzie also failed, sometime later, to notice that the noises had now ceased. She was, by that time, staring at a picture of Frank taken just after his twelfth birthday, with his new bicycle. She remembered it had been a splendid dark green. Standing behind the beaming Frank was Billy Pierce and the rest of the gang. Right at the back and to the side was a tall, skinny girl with wild, frizzy hair. Lizzie touched the small face, remembering, even now, how much she had hated having that hair combed through. Scanning the youthful faces, she recognised and could put names to more than half their number. Not bad going after all these years, she thought. When this had been taken, she was the only girl in the gang and she always dressed just like one of the boys. That hair of hers was the only clue that the tearaway in baggy dungarees might perhaps be female. It was clear, seeing the photographic evidence, that Lizzie had occupied a very junior rank in the tree-climbing gang. Being a girl, she had probably been tolerated because she was a tomboy, but also and more importantly, because she was Frank's sister and Frank was very definitely the leader.

Frank had wanted her to join, so the rest had shrugged their assent and accepted her with varying degrees of lack of enthusiasm.

Lizzie eventually shut the album and lifted it up to its niche on the shelf by the window. As the large book slid into place, a sudden movement out in the garden attracted her attention. She turned quickly, in time to see someone creeping low around the corner of the house. That man again. Lizzie grasped the key at her neck. Thank goodness May was safe inside. Lizzie's recent desire to tease May evaporated instantly in the face of this shared danger. She quickly leant back, away from the window. A bush had moved. He was coming back. Safely hidden behind the blind, Lizzie watched as he crept slowly across the lawn. At first she couldn't see his face but then he glanced over his shoulder, looking almost exactly at her window. He hadn't seen her but Lizzie had certainly seen him, and not for the first time. Those wide set, grey eyes. It was the man who had claimed to be a police officer.

Lizzie felt sick.

Her hand at her stomach, she sat down heavily, her mind in turmoil. What should she do? To summon any help, she would have to get past the man and out into the lane. She might just make it, but did she dare? She heard the loud click of a handle. The front door. He was trying to get in. Lizzie hurriedly scanned the room and found what she was looking for; the poker resting in the fireplace. Wincing at its scraping noise as she dragged it across the hearth, Lizzie heaved it up and weighed it in her hand. The poker was heavy, perhaps too heavy for her to wield effectively, but it might well act as a deterrent. She stood still now and listened. She could hear nothing but the pounding of her own heartbeat. Poker raised, she crept over to the door and slowly turned the handle.

Opening the door only two or three inches, she peered out. The staircase blocked her view of most of the hall so, listening hard, she opened the door a little wider. She held her breath as she stepped out.

At first the silence was reassuring: it didn't look like he had managed to get into the house. But then Lizzie realised that she couldn't hear May either. May had obviously abandoned the inevitably fruitless search for the back door key, but what was she doing now? Had she seen the man too? Was she hiding somewhere, trying to stay quiet?

Lizzie tiptoed across the silent hall, then slowly sidled along the corridor towards May's room. Once there, she opened the door without knocking, not wanting to make any unnecessary noise. She stuck her head into the room and May looked up, startled.

Before May could reprove her for the intrusion, Lizzie put her finger to her lips.

"Shh! Stay here, May. Just stay here."

May looked confused but Lizzie had to act quickly. She couldn't waste time.

"Just stay in your room."

"Alright, but -"

"No time for buts. Stay here and stay quiet. OK?"

Not waiting for a reply, Lizzie closed May's door and crossed the hall. She had determined to go for help but, before risking opening the front door, she peered through the frosted glass of the window to its side. There was no sign of movement out there. Was it safe to venture out? Perhaps, Lizzie thought, it would be wise to check the whole garden before risking it. The view was best from the windows upstairs. Accordingly she went up to the landing, this time carefully avoiding the two squeaky treads. She went to all of the first floor windows in turn, but couldn't see the man anywhere in the garden. Perhaps he'd gone. Lizzie hardly dared hope that he had. But if he had, what should she do? How long should she wait before going into town for help? And indeed, what help could she get? If he had gone, there was little anyone could now do besides offer reassurance. But Lizzie didn't want platitudes; she wanted action. She wanted him taken 'off the streets', as the papers had it, for a long, long stretch. For him to be caught, he had still to be here when the police came, so, awful though the prospect was, she had to hope he was still out there.

By the time she had made her way back to the front door, she had convinced herself that he was indeed still somewhere in the garden. Again, she peered out of the frosted glass. Still no sign of him.

Summoning up all her courage, Lizzie opened the front door, just wide enough for her to peep out and scan the path. It was clear. She had to take her chance. She had to fetch help and get this man caught. Her hand flexed around the comforting grip of the poker. She gently pushed the door and was relieved at just how quietly she was able to close it again behind her. So far, so good. She scanned the garden ahead of her and went carefully down the uneven steps to the path. She almost cried out in shock at the crunch of gravel under her feet. What a racket! Shifting her weight back onto the foot still resting on the lowest step, she carefully lifted the other foot out of the gravel and onto the grass. Had that single footstep been enough to attract his attention? Should she turn and run back to the house? No. She wouldn't be fast enough up those steps and she wouldn't be able to unlock the door quickly enough either. She had no choice, she would have to stand and fight. She still had the poker in her hand and she would do her best to put it to good and injurious use before she was overwhelmed. She braced herself for an attack, which, thankfully, did not come.

After a few tense moments it was clear to Lizzie that she was safe, for now. Still keeping a sharp look out, she crept towards the gate. The track into town was clear but the trees that had so prettily framed it in the bright sunlight on Monday now seemed only to offer hiding places for possible attackers. And the track itself seemed to stretch an eternity to its ending on Oak Street. Trembling with anxiety, Lizzie took one more look back towards the house. May's worried face was at the window. Lizzie flashed her what she hoped was a reassuring smile and signalled for her to keep away from the window, then she turned and began the long walk to Oak Street, with each snap of a fallen twig, each rustle of leaves or cry of a bird causing her to jump in terror. On several occasions she nearly dropped the heavy poker in her fright. She was thoroughly shaken, her nerves frayed and raw.

When she reached Oak Street, Lizzie felt a terrific surge of relief wash over her at having reached the end of the track in unexpected safety. The tension in her body, that had till now been carrying her along, masking any weakness in her limbs, fell away all at once, leaving her suddenly weak and unsure. Her legs began to tremble and she felt feverish though her hands and feet were icy cold. She was exhausted and her fatigue, acting in conjunction with the intense, visceral fear, seemed to be disconnecting and distancing her from her surroundings. Everything around her, the quiet houses, their tidy gardens, was as it always was; but Lizzie felt herself slipping into a state of increasingly crippling disorientation.

The man hadn't been hiding behind the trees along the track, so where was he? Was he watching her right now, stalking, waiting to strike? Or was he still back at the house. With poor May. May was in danger. Should she go back? Should she go on and get help? Her initial decisiveness was now failing her. She stood, swaying slightly, in the middle of the paved area where once she had scrambled about in the wonderful old oak. If only she had that freedom and agility still. If only she could escape back to those happy times.

Her mind was wandering and for a few brief seconds Lizzie was lost in her memories.

However, urgent thoughts and images soon broke through; a man was in the garden! He was trying to get into the house. May was in danger. Lizzie had to get moving. Though she was feeling desperately weak, she had to push herself on. She had to get help.

As she stumbled on, the world continued to shrink around her. She found herself becoming aware of each ragged breath and, though she tried to move quickly, her pace was still far too slow. She was tiring more with every laboured step and, within a few minutes, any movement had become a huge effort, her limbs leaden, as if battling to wade through treacle. There was still no one in sight. Lizzie staggered along Oak Street to the corner, her entire body now shaking and her mind struggling in vain against overwhelming anxiety. She could focus on just one aim now: get help, she must get help.

She was beginning to feel very cold. Any sounds around her were becoming increasingly muffled and, in the ensuing silence, her vision seemed also to be closing in, so that she was aware only of the small area of ground directly in front of her shuffling feet. That tiny patch of paving soon became her whole world. Just a few more steps, just a few more and she would surely be at the end of the road. Could she make it that far? Terrified and tearful, Lizzie was beginning to doubt it. Her heart was racing in full panic and the silence of the world around her was fast becoming drowned in the roaring pulse pounding in her ears. Her chest was tightening. She couldn't breathe. Pain, the like of which she had never known before, was burning through her, tearing at her. The roaring in her ears was deafening now. Her head was swimming.

"Miss Oatley?" a small child's piping voice.

Mildly irritated, Beth Oatley looked up from her book to see who had called her. Little Danny Smith was running towards her, across the school yard.

"What is it Daniel?"

"Look, Miss Oatley, the old lady."

Puzzled, Beth followed Danny across to the chain link fence. Once there she was just in time to see, on the other side of the road, Lizzie falling, first to her knees and then down, onto her side, to lie forlorn and crumpled on the ground. Danny and the other children surveyed the scene in solemn silence.

Lizzie was unaware of the interest her fall had generated in the school yard, indeed she was unconscious of everything for several minutes more. In that short time Beth Oatley acted quickly; the children were herded back into class, medical help was called and Beth herself came across the road to the old woman.

When Lizzie opened her eyes, both she and Beth started with surprise.

Lizzie didn't know where she was or why she was lying here on the ground. And who was this young woman leaning over her? Lizzie made an effort to rise, but Beth eased her back down. The young woman smiled, warm with self-congratulation; proud of the way she was handling this little emergency. Her prompt and decisive action could well have saved this old woman's life. She continued to bestow a beatific smile upon the old lady, all the while making soft cooing sounds as you might to a frightened child, but Beth Oatley's mind was elsewhere.

Daydreaming, Beth was already imagining the front page of next week's local newspaper, her own face smiling out; the reluctant local heroine modestly dismissing the editor's glowing praise. She supposed that there might perhaps also be a smaller picture of this frail old woman, with accompanying text spelling out her gratitude in quietly understated terms, along the lines of, 'Miss Elizabeth Oatley (22) is a modern day Good Samaritan, an angel. Her calm and prompt actions undoubtedly saved my life'. All of Beth Oatley's family and friends would see it and, more importantly, her colleagues would see it. No more treating her as the department Junior, no more trivialising her ideas for change. Everyone would treat her with more respect from now on.

Beth had always delighted in grandiose imaginings, but she had never had the gift of an event like this come her way. She couldn't believe her good fortune and she owed it to this poor old lady. Gently, she lifted Lizzie's hand and stroked it as she smiled her most benign and reassuring smile.

At first, Lizzie was confused and content to let this stranger take control, but then that insistent, far away thought came seeping back.

"I must get help," she gasped.

"Help's on the way. Just lie still."

Beth was accustomed to soothing the most tearful and fractious of six-year-olds. She was using those same honeyed tones now to calm the old woman who seemed otherwise to be in danger of becoming unnecessarily agitated. Perhaps she was in pain, or injured by the fall. Beth couldn't tell.

"I must get help." Lizzie gasped again, trying to get up.

Beth gently, but firmly, pushed her back down.

"Help is coming."

The honey was less noticeable now.

Lizzie was becoming desperate.

"No, I must get help."

She was struggling to sit up and becoming increasingly irritated by this young woman's persistent and forcible solicitude. When Beth again tried, gently but firmly, to push her back down, Lizzie scowled.

"Get your hands off me, young woman," she snapped, pulling her hand out of the young woman's with a sharp tug, "I have to get help."

Biting her lip, Beth gave up. She would have to let this argumentative and, frankly, ungrateful, old woman sit herself up. Beth was aggrieved. This was not how it was supposed to go. The rescue services and perhaps a local reporter or two should by now have arrived to find the wonderfully photogenic young teacher selflessly tending the helpless, unconscious old woman. At this rate, the old crone would be on her feet and long gone by the time the paramedics and reporters put in an appearance. So Beth was guiltily delighted and hugely relieved when Lizzie suddenly fainted again with the exertion. Beth caught and supported the old woman's head. Then, with Lizzie once again prone, Beth took her hand again and continued its tender stoking. Lizzie woke and opened her eyes briefly, but was too exhausted to resist.

Beth Oatley scanned the roads, willing the ambulance, and the reporter, to appear before Lizzie woke up again.

8

Eyes still closed, Lizzie was dimly aware of a conversation going on above her head

"Just leave it to us, miss. We'll take it from here." Someone was insisting and with some authority.

Then another voice, oh no, that annoying young woman.

"I think I should come with her."

"Are you her daughter?"

"No, I'm a teacher over th-"

"Then you'll have to let us take it from here. OK? Thank you, lady, have a nice day."

Doors clunked shut, then they were moving and Lizzie's world slipped briefly back into darkness.

Once at the hospital she began to revive as the medical staff worked around her. She had the wit to lie to them about having been unconscious for the few moments after the fall. She wanted to get out as soon as possible. Nevertheless, they assessed her as a 'watch and wait' case and then left her in a quiet corner of the otherwise apparently chaotic room. With mounting frustration, she asked and kept on asking, to speak to someone in authority, the police, anyone who could help May. The nurses were kindly, but a viral outbreak at the hospital had left them chronically understaffed and each was desperately busy. With distracted promises to 'be back soon' they hurried past, dismissing her pleas as the inconsequential flotsam of a disoriented mind. Such confusion was entirely to be expected in the circumstances. Only when Lizzie, now panicking, struggled to leave, did they finally stop and listen to what she actually had to say. A police officer was immediately summoned and, through frantic tears, Lizzie told him about the man and her own escape from the house. When she told him that May was still trapped in the house, he became suddenly animated and at once called for a patrol car to drive over and check that May was safe.

"They'll call me as soon they have anything and I'll let you know straight away, " he said, "but, for now, just let the doctors do their tests then try to get some rest, Miss Atwell."

His voice was persuasive and Lizzie was bone weary, but she couldn't just lie there. She had to protect May. She had to get back home. But, though she tried to raise herself up, she no longer had the energy. Her arms began to shake alarmingly and she slumped back onto the pillows, despair and frustration closing over her. She had no choice now. She would have to trust May's safety to others. She would have to rely on the police to save her.

After all these years of responsibility, that was hard to accept.

Very hard.

The police officer was true to his word and, within half an hour, came back to tell her that the patrol car had reported from the house. May was safe but the man had gone. They were going to keep a watch on May and the house for a while, so Lizzie wasn't to worry any more. No worries anymore? That was too much to hope for.

But Lizzie did relax a little at the news and she could feel her strength beginning to build up once more.

The doctor later returned to explain the outcome of her tests. She spoke to Lizzie for some time, but Lizzie heard only snatches of what was said: she hadn't broken any bones; she wasn't in any immediate danger; it had been a warning, not a big time heart attack but a warning; the doctors were not overly concerned. In short, Lizzie heard only what she wanted to hear and closed her ears to all the rest. She thanked the doctor but politely declined her offer to find Lizzie a bed in the hospital for a few day's observation. She would recover more quickly in her own home.

The doctor tried at some length to dissuade her, but in vain.

"Please reconsider, Miss Atwell." she urged finally, "It would only be for a day or so, just so that we can keep an eye on you."

Lizzie quite liked this woman, she didn't patronise and she genuinely seemed to care, but Lizzie had to get back to May. Her mind was made up and, when she spoke, her voice was firm.

"Thank you for your concern, doctor. You're very kind, but I want to go home." She looked directly at the doctor and added, "I take full responsibility for any consequences."

The doctor pursed her lips and looked at Lizzie thoughtfully. There was a moment's silence then she raised her eyebrows and shrugged.

"Very well, Miss Atwell. You seem to be fully competent so I guess you're entitled to make that decision. I'll sort out the paperwork."

Soon Lizzie was on the pay-phone near the hospital's main entrance, calling a taxi. The doctor, touched by the old woman's determination and realising that Lizzie had no handbag or purse with her, had insisted that she take enough money to pay for a ride home. All she asked in return was that Lizzie promise to make some changes so as to take things a little easier in future. Lizzie smiled and, out of necessity, accepted the money, but she didn't actually make the promise. She didn't want to lie. The doctor was a decent human being and there weren't many of those left as far as Lizzie could judge. Also Lizzie would never make a promise that she didn't intend to keep and she didn't see how she could change any aspect in her life. Once the man was arrested and sent to prison she and May would simply slip back into their accustomed ways.

Thankfully, the doctor took Lizzie's smile for assent and didn't press the matter further.

The gum-chewing cab driver had to ask Lizzie for directions to the lane. In four years driving for the company he'd never known there was a house down there. He turned off Oak Street and they bumped slowly along the lane's uneven surface, the driver wincing with every bounce.

"D'ya get much traffic down here, lady?" he asked through gritted teeth.

"I think you might be the first," Lizzie replied, with a smile.

She was becoming steadily more composed as she neared her home and when, from a distance, she saw the police patrol car parked outside the house her fears were further allayed.

The patrol car had a very different effect on the cab driver.

"Hey, what's going on here?" he asked, frowning at Lizzie in the rear view mirror, "You in some kinda trouble?"

"No, no." Lizzie assured him, "We had a break in, an intruder."

The driver shook his head.

"Lotta that goes on these days." he sympathised, relieved that his fare was not just about to get herself arrested and involve him in an unpleasant and possibly dangerous incident. She looked at first like any other sweet little old lady, but who could tell? Paying recklessly scant attention to the road's ruts and potholes, he snatched glances in the rear view mirror, studying Lizzie's features. He decided that behind that genteel mask there might be a lady who could be guilty of something. Poisoning perhaps? Yeah, she could be the sweet little old lady who poisons her neighbours and any unfortunate doorstep salesmen with a winning smile and a few drops of arsenic in their tea. Camomile tea...

He shook himself back to reality as they pulled up outside the house. The old woman paid the fare, thanked him civilly then walked carefully up the path. She didn't look back, she didn't need any help and he was in no hurry to get involved with the police, so he turned with as much speed as the suspension-wrecking ruts in the lane would allow and headed back into town.

Lizzie was also in a hurry. All her feelings of frustration and irritation towards May, which had led to this morning's cat and mouse game, had been pushed aside. Lizzie now just wanted to see May again, to be assured that she was really safe. She walked briskly up the path and had the keys ready in her hand before she'd even climbed the steps. She unlocked and opened the door with even more than her usual haste and rushed into the hall.

"May? May? Where are you?"

"Oh Lizzie, thank goodness! I'm here in the kitchen, dear."

The sound of May's voice lifted the last burden of anxiety from Lizzie's shoulders. She almost ran to the kitchen, flinging open the door then, with a gasp, she stopped dead in her tracks.

May was sitting at the table, sharing a pot of tea with him: the man.

He was in a police uniform as he had been the other evening and his cold grey eyes lifted to meet Lizzie's as she burst into the room. He didn't look away but held her gaze, quizzically tilting his head as she stared, stunned with the shock of the unexpected. Lizzie may have stopped dead, but she felt as if her brain had continued in motion, crashing into the front of her skull. Utter confusion. She couldn't say, or do, anything. Her mouth opened but no sound came out.

The silence stretched out awkwardly. It was finally broken by the man.

"Are you OK, Miss Atwell?"

He stood up and came towards her. Lizzie backed away. He looked concerned.

'God he's good at this act,' Lizzie thought.

"Will you let me help you Miss Atwell?" he asked, an arm outstretched.

Lizzie was still unable to speak. She looked from May to the man and back again, bewildered.

Now May was looking worried.

"Are you alright Lizzie? You look very pale, dear. Please sit down."

Almost automatically, used to a lifetime of trying to appease May, Lizzie found herself sitting down as requested, although part of her brain cried out against it.

May glanced up at the man, seeking reassurance. Lizzie was shocked. She felt betrayed by that glance: May should look to her for reassurance, not to this stranger. Seeing May look up to him, Lizzie felt isolated, as if they were in league against her.

"Lizzie?" May ventured, "Are you sure you should have come out of hospital so soon?"

The man was nodding.

"Yes, ma'am. Perhaps you should have stayed in, if only for a rest." he said, his voice oily with concern, "I could give you a lift back to the hospital if you'd like."

'Oh yes, you'd like that wouldn't you?' thought Lizzie. It was obvious to her that he wanted to separate them. May would be defenceless against him if she were left alone here in the house. What was his game? Was he going to rob them? She almost hoped his motives were that simple, the alternatives, gleaned from her readings at the library and the news stand, were too awful to contemplate. Her mind was whirling with fears and wild imaginings.

Again, May and the man exchanged glances.

He moved another step closer to Lizzie.

"Keep away from me!" she squeaked.

She hadn't meant to squeak like that, but he had frightened her, creeping towards her, for all the world like a spider advancing on its paralysed prey. There was a dreadful inevitability about his approach, as if she might as well give up now and accept his mastery over their fate. It was almost mesmerising.

But she shook herself. No, it wasn't going to be that simple. She wasn't going to make it easy for him. She wasn't yet sure how best to react, but she had a notion that she shouldn't give too much away. Slowly, as her brain began to impose some order, she distilled the reasoning behind this: the man probably didn't know that she had seen him clearly in the garden and recognised him as the prowler. She had to try to act calmly and not let him realise that she saw through his disguise. If he found out what she knew, he might panic and act hastily. He might attack them right there and then. Lizzie suppressed a shudder. She needed to think of a plan. She had to play for time. With huge effort, she forced her face into a trembling smile.

"I'm sorry, Officer. It's just that everyone at the hospital has been making such a fuss of me and I'm not used to it. I don't like it." she managed, the strain in her voice lending credibility to the hesitant words.

The man stopped.

"I quite understand, Miss Atwell."

He turned back towards May.

"If your sister's alright, Miss May, I should leave and let you both get some rest."

Lizzie held her breath. Was it really going to be this easy?

Then May spoke up and nearly ruined everything.

"Oh," she begged, her voice dull with disappointment, "there's no need for you to hurry away, is there Officer? My sister is always worrying about burglars and that sort of thing. I'm sure we'd both love for you to stay with us a little longer. Perhaps another cup of tea?"

Lizzie's eyes were wide in disbelief. What was May thinking? He was ready to leave, for God's sake be quiet and let him go.

The man turned from May to face Lizzie, the grey eyes unblinking, holding her gaze with that probing stare of his. What on earth was going on behind those eyes? Lizzie couldn't tell and didn't like to guess. She made her smile wider, fighting to steady the trembling at the margins of her mouth, her facial muscles tightening into aching knots. She felt sure her face must look manic rather than serenely innocent, but, right now, this crazy smile was the best she could do.

"Thank you no. I think I should probably be on my way, that's if you're sure you're OK, Miss Atwell?"

"Yes, yes, I'm fine, really," said Lizzie with desperate jollity, "I just need a rest." and, turning to May, "The officer must have a lot of other work to be getting on with. We mustn't be selfish and keep him from his duties elsewhere, now must we?"

Hidden behind the man, May stuck her head to one side to see past him. She scowled at Lizzie, but Lizzie ignored the look and pre-empted any further outburst from her by suggesting that the man let her show him to the door. At first he demurred, insisting that he could see himself out, but Lizzie wanted to see him out of the house, to know for sure that he had gone. She was insistent, smiling again, the very picture of a courteous, if somewhat intense, hostess. He raised his hands, acknowledging that it would be pointless to argue further. He motioned to Lizzie to lead the way, but, before following her out of the kitchen, he thanked May for the tea and wished her well. That May was so obviously taken in by his show of manners annoyed Lizzie intensely, until she remembered that she had been duped in exactly the same way on first meeting him. She had even thought him fine and handsome at first.

Now, walking ahead of him, towards the front door, Lizzie's every nerve was alert. What if he attacked her now, from behind? Would she be able to do anything to defend herself? Probably the only factor in her favour was that he wouldn't expect her to have anticipated his move. Perhaps that foresight would buy her a few precious seconds in which to do…What?

She fought to conceal her anxiety. She must be brave. She had to get him away out of the house but, with fear of an attack at every step, her walk to the door was daunting and seemed interminable. When finally she reached and grasped the door handle, she opened the door and spun about, rather too quickly, to face him. He nearly bumped into her and she cried out in surprise.

'So much for being braced for attack' she thought.

It was some comfort that he was as taken aback as she was. She hastily stood aside to let him pass.

"You're sure you'll be OK now?" he asked, yet again, his show of concern looking almost genuine.

"Yes, I'm fine, I'm fine. Thank you Officer. Goodbye."

He raised an eyebrow at the abruptness of her leave-taking, but he said nothing more and left the house, treading lightly down the steps. He walked out to his car. The car! Lizzie only then remembered the patrol car. How could he have a patrol car if he wasn't...? Dear God. He was a real police officer.

Without waiting to see him drive off, Lizzie shut and locked the door then collapsed into the chair. What did this mean? Well, for one thing, if he was a real policeman then she couldn't go to the police for help again: she couldn't know if he was acting alone or if there were other officers at the station also involved. Lizzie closed her eyes and trawled back through her memories of the day, trying to remember exactly what she had said to the other police officer, in the hospital. That officer's notes would be held in some file or other at the police station, where others would be able to read it. How much had she said?

May broke into Lizzie's effort of concentration.

"Well, I must say, I think you were rather rude to him, Lizzie." she said, heedless of Lizzie's vexed look."

"Be quiet while I think," Lizzie snapped.

"No, I won't be quiet, I won't." May's words were tumbling out, "This has been an absolutely dreadful day and that nice young man helped me tremendously." Lizzie raised her eyes towards the ceiling, but May continued,

"You probably don't realise just how worried I was. First I was told was that you were at the hospital: that you'd collapsed in the street. And I still don't know why you had to rush off like that in the first place, without so much as a goodbye. You're always so secretive, but you really should tell me where you're going when you go out. I didn't know where you were and I thought you might be…ill…or badly hurt…or anything. And then they said someone had been snooping about." May had slowed down, words rolling out more gently now that her emotion was spent. She stopped and there was a moment's silence between them. May's chest rose and fell as she took in and sighed out a deep, deep breath. "Lizzie," she whispered at last, "when you left I was all alone and I was so very frightened."

Almost silently, May started to cry.

Lizzie sat for a moment, watching her poor sister weep; huge tears sliding from those lovely hazel eyes. She never could bear to see May cry and so, even now, when she should have been telling May everything, making her understand, Lizzie simply reached out and took May's hand in hers.

"It's alright, May. Don't cry. Shhh now."

May leant forward, let her walking stick fall to the floor and put her arms around Lizzie's shoulders. Lizzie, still seated, wrapped her arms around May and held her close.

"I had a fall, but I'm OK and I'm home now. Everything's going to be alright." she soothed.

'But was it?' She wondered, keeping the thought to herself.

Then, softly, "Shhh now, May, shhh."

It took several minutes for Lizzie to calm her sister. During that time, May said nothing and expected no words from Lizzie: she simply needed the physical reassurance. Lizzie's mind was therefore free to wander elsewhere. She knew that she could never fully share with her sister. Theirs was not a partnership of equals. May was a child. She would, of course, have to be told that the man was not who he appeared to be and she would have to understand that he was never to be allowed back into their house. But Lizzie wouldn't be able to confide her deeper fears as to the nature of his intentions. She would somehow have to protect them both from him, and she would have to do it alone.

Still hugging her sister close, Lizzie stared blankly ahead, seeing nothing, her thoughts far away.

9

Picking up May's walking stick, Lizzie eased herself to her feet, gently loosening May's grip around her neck as she did so. She passed the cane to May and supported her as they made their way back to the kitchen.

Once there, after settling May in a chair, she set to making a pot of tea. Standing at the sink, Lizzie replayed the events of the day in her mind. It occurred to her that the day and their immediate situation here in the kitchen perfectly summed up the norms of their lifelong relationship. It was she who had been alert to the threat, seen the intruder and then risked her own safety in going for help for May who, as ever, had no idea what was going on. In her efforts to protect her little sister, Lizzie had ended up in hospital. May, on the other hand, had remained comfortably safe, sheltered in the house and, in spite of unwittingly entertaining the very man who threatened them, had been cheerfully ignorant of any risk. And yet, after all her exertions and bravery, it was Lizzie who was now comforting May, Lizzie who was making tea, Lizzie who was being mother.

Lizzie prided herself that she rarely, if ever, gave way to self-pity, but just now she would have loved to have someone mothering her.

She bit her lip and looked down. The kettle was

overflowing into the sink.

As they sat together at the kitchen table, May, restored by the hot tea, began to chatter away in her usual fashion. The officer's name was Michael Lowry and he was a very well-spoken and polite young man. He'd been sent to check that she was alright because they'd heard that Lizzie was in hospital, but also that someone had been seen lurking in the area. Once Michael had assured himself that May was safe he had kept her company while she waited for news of Lizzie. They'd chatted for what seemed like hours. Such a pleasant young man, his mother must be so very proud. In fact, May had actually said that to him, but he'd just shrugged off all her praise and said that he was just doing his job.

"So, you see Lizzie," she said finally, "he was very kind to me today and he really didn't deserve for you to be so short with him."

It was only a gentle rebuke. May didn't want to upset her sister because she knew that, whatever Lizzie did, it was always with the very best of intentions. May perhaps hoped that Lizzie would nod in acknowledgment. That little gesture would have been enough for her.

But Lizzie seemed not even to have noticed her sister's mild criticism. She had let May finish and now wanted to take her back over the details.

"What did you talk about with him, May?"

May, though disappointed at the lack of an apology, was also intrigued. Why did Lizzie want to know what they'd spoken about? Why did it matter? May was quiet for a moment, thinking back. Had anything been said in those few hours that was of particular interest or importance? If anything had been, she had by now forgotten it and, if she'd already forgotten it then it couldn't have been that interesting in the first place, now could it?

"We just chatted." she shrugged.

"Yes, but what about?" Lizzie persisted.

"Well, nothing really."

But, from the expectant look on Lizzie's face, May could tell that this was not going to be enough. She would have to try harder to remember. Frowning, she took another sip of tea, playing for time. Lizzie seemed content to wait, but kept up an intense stare that put May very much under pressure.

"He said...Oh yes, he said that we have a beautiful home. And he said he thought it must take a lot of work to keep a place like this going, but I told him that we'd always lived here and we were used to it, so it doesn't seem like hard work to us. And, let's see, I told him about our vegetable plot and the orchard."

"And was he interested in any of that?" Lizzie interrupted.

"Well, yes dear. I told you, he's a very personable young man. He was interested in everything. He asked about you."

"Why, what did he say?"

"Let me see. Oh yes. I told him that you do all the shopping because of my arthritis." Lizzie raised an eyebrow but, if May remembered yesterday's fraught conversation, she gave no indication of it. "And he said he was sorry that it's so difficult for me to get around. Then I explained that's why my room's down here instead of upstairs, like yours."

Lizzie was growing impatient. She had to get May to focus.

"You said he asked about me. What did he want to know?"

"He wasn't really asking questions. He just said that he wanted to be sure that you were alright because, and you won't believe this, he was the police officer who came here the other night. He said you'd looked a bit unsettled when he saw you then and he was worried about you. I'm surprised you didn't recognise him today."

"I did."

May made the familiar half-smile that told Lizzie she didn't believe her.

"I did recognise him." Lizzie insisted flatly.

"Then why were you so rude to him?" asked May, quietly triumphant.

It was very rare for May to feel that she had got the better of Lizzie in any argument. But, on this occasion, she believed that the evidence was in her favour. Lizzie obviously hadn't recognised Michael or she wouldn't have spoken so rudely to him. Lizzie would surely have to admit that she hadn't recognised him at all. But why had she lied about it? After all, there's no disgrace in not remembering someone you've met only once and in the dark.

May sighed. She realised that Lizzie wouldn't answer her question. Lizzie would rather remain silent than admit she was wrong about anything. She always had to be right and May had often wondered why that was. Lizzie was a wonderful person, quite wonderful, but no one could be right all the time and what an awful strain it must be, forever struggling to live up to this impossible expectation of perfection. May would have loved to be able to persuade Lizzie to drop some of the worries that she heaped upon herself. Most of all May wished that she could actually say these things to Lizzie. She had tried, occasionally and without much success in the past, but now, here in the kitchen at the end of a very strange and difficult day, it was certainly not the right time to try again. Her hope was that, someday, she would be able to convince Lizzie of the basic goodness of people and the happiness that was there to be enjoyed in the everyday tasks of their settled, peaceful life. How wonderful it would be if, one day, Lizzie would listen and allow herself to relax, even if only a little.

Lizzie did indeed ignore not only May's question but also the hint of triumph in her sister's voice. May could believe her or not, it wasn't important, but Lizzie naturally had no intention of saying she'd failed to recognise the man. As if she would ever be able to forget that face with its cold, wide set eyes. Lizzie was otherwise occupied: trying to judge how much she should tell May about the man. She took a breath and began.

"May, listen to me. The police officer-"

"Michael, Officer Michael Lowry." May interjected helpfully.

Lizzie started again, this time wearing a look intended forcefully to discourage any further interruptions.

"You said he told you that someone had been seen prowling around?" May gave a nod in response. "Well," Lizzie continued, "I was the one who saw the prowler." She saw the look of surprise come over May's face. "That's why I left in such a hurry. I went to get help. I had a fall before I got to town but, as soon as I could, I got someone to come out to make sure you were safe."

Forgetting her momentary sense of triumph, and moved by Lizzie's selfless devotion, May reached forward and touched Lizzie's arm in a tender expression of gratitude.

"The thing is, May," Lizzie added after a moment, "it was him: Officer Lowry. It was him I saw prowling around the garden."

Lizzie had expected a look of shock but, instead, May looked relieved.

"Of course he was in the garden." she said, "Once he'd made sure I was alright, he searched the whole place.

He was looking for the prowler. Goodness Lizzie, for an awful moment I thought you were trying to say that Michael was the prowler." May smiled at such a ludicrous thought.

"May," said Lizzie, "think about it. You saw him search the garden **after** I went to town to raise the alarm. But I saw him creeping round the garden before. That's why I left to get help. May, he is the prowler."

May shook her head.

"No, Lizzie, I know you. I know how fearless you are; you'd have confronted him, right there in the kitchen, if he were the prowler. When you got back and saw him here, you'd have said something, wouldn't you, Lizzie?"

May was looking for reassurance in Lizzie's face, but, finding none, her own face began to cloud over with uncertainty. Lizzie said nothing and simply returned May's stare, but her continued silence was eloquent. Gradually, May grasped its implications.

"Do you mean that I've been sitting here all afternoon with a prowler? Here, in our own kitchen?"

Lizzie nodded, "I should have told you that he was in the garden before I left this morning. I'm sorry May."

May looked quizzical.

"Why didn't you tell me?"

"There wasn't time."

May raised her eyebrows but said no more. There followed an awkward silence during which May absently ran her fingers back and forth over the tablecloth, smoothing out non-existent creases. Suddenly her hands were stilled, palms down, on the table. She looked up.

"No," she said, "I'm sorry, Lizzie, but I can't believe it. You must be mistaken. I simply can't believe that such a nice young man could be capable of prowling around like that. No, you must be mistaken, Lizzie. You must be."

"May?"

"No, Lizzie, I'm not listening to any more of this. I believe you think you saw someone in the garden, fine, but I'm absolutely certain it couldn't have been Michael. You don't know what he's like. You couldn't hope to meet a kinder, more helpful young man. You must be mistaken." May put up her hand to pre-empt a response from Lizzie. "No, Lizzie, no more. I've heard enough. I need to go and lie down."

As May left the room, Lizzie told herself that she would give May a few hours to think over what she'd been told. It was a lot to take in, but May would come round. In the meantime, what was Lizzie to do?

It was getting dark now, too late to go back into town to get help. But even if it were still daylight out there, whom could she turn to for that help, if she couldn't trust the police? The seclusion of their house, previously a source of delight, seemed suddenly a worrying cause of anxiety: no longer seclusion, but isolation. And theirs was not solely a physical isolation. Lizzie and May had allowed themselves to become isolated on a personal level too. Did they know anyone in the town? Lizzie might still be able to recall the names of Frank's old gang, but how many of them were still in the area? Those that hadn't already died had mostly moved miles away to be nearer their grandchildren. May never saw anyone of course, but was she, Lizzie, any better?

Her twice-weekly trips into town had made her a familiar figure by which people could set their mental calendars. Her routine was always the same and yet she hadn't struck up a lasting friendship with anyone in all these years. People who crossed her path during her Monday and Friday trips had grown accustomed to seeing an old lady who liked to keep herself to herself. Respectable, perhaps even a little aloof, but probably pleasant enough if you got to know her. The problem was that nobody had. Lizzie's frosty demeanour had, consciously or otherwise, deterred everyone from making that vital initial contact. And one consequence of all those years of haughty independence was that there was now no one to whom Lizzie felt she could turn for help.

She would have to deal with this herself. She thought around the problem as she began her evening routine of securing the house and decided that her first move, first thing tomorrow, would be to have new locks put in. These old ones had been in place for years. There must surely be better, stronger locks available now. First thing in the morning she would go to Billy Pierce's store and buy new locks for all the doors and windows. Making that first decision gave Lizzie's spirits a boost, but the glow faded quickly with the realisation that a long night stretched out ahead of her. Just knowing that he had been here, in their house, would be enough to make sleep very difficult for her, so she decided that she might as well stay dressed and alert rather than go to bed. If anything happened, if, God forbid, he were to come back, she would be ready.

Grim-faced she made her way to the kitchen and took the knife out of the drawer.

As Lizzie had expected, the night was a long, dark and lonely one. But it was also without incident and the first watery light, preceding the full warmth of dawn, found her dozing in the hard-backed chair by the front door.

Awake now, she had slept a little in snatches throughout her vigil but her body ached and her head was throbbing painfully. Squinting to shield her eyes, though the pale light was still dim, Lizzie made her way to the kitchen. She took a couple of aspirin and shivered as the icy water ran down her throat. Then, sitting at the kitchen table, head in hands, she waited for her head to clear.

Throughout the night she had been trying to organise her thoughts. Try as she might, she couldn't remember exactly what she'd said to the police officer at the hospital, so she had to assume the worst: that she had told him everything. By now Officer Lowry could well have read his fellow officer's report and would know that she had seen him prowling in the garden. Only Lowry would know that he had been recognised; anyone else reading the report would believe, as Lizzie had, that the prowler was someone impersonating a police officer. What would Lowry do?

Lizzie tried to imagine herself in his place. What would she do? It would all depend, she reasoned, on whether he thought that other people would believe the word of an old lady more readily than that of a police officer. Perversely, it was with some relief that she decided that most people would probably believe him and dismiss her version of events as fantasy. If Lowry reasoned in the same way then she might stand a chance: he might not think it worth his while trying to silence her.

She had to hope that his mind worked along the same lines as her own, but, just in case that hope was misplaced, she determined to write down all she knew about him. Had she not been without sleep for most of the night, she might have seen this as a rather melodramatic plan, but to Lizzie now, sitting alone in the chill light of early morning, it seemed no more than sensible precaution.

She shuffled over to the dresser and took out her writing paper and pen. It would be more than two hours before the hardware store opened. She had time to write everything down in a letter and then hide it somewhere safe, somewhere he would never think to look for it.

10

Lizzie had finished the letter and sealed it in an envelope with May's name clearly written on the front. She was now wandering the house looking for a safe place in which to hide it. Her difficulty was that, if she thought that a particular box, drawer, or top shelf would make a safe hiding place for her evidence, then it immediately seemed obvious that Lowry would think of looking there too. She wasn't thinking clearly, she was well aware of that. She was so very tired, but she knew she had to hide the letter away before she left the house. Her mind was focused on her task to such an extent that she failed to register that May was awake, indeed that she was now standing in the hall, watching her, a puzzled expression spreading over her face.

"What are you doing?" May asked.

"I'm looking for something."

"What?"

"Nothing. Just leave it, will you?"

"If you tell me what you've lost I can help you look for it, dear."

"It's nothing. No look, if you really want to do something to help, go make some coffee. I haven't started breakfast yet; I've been too busy."

"Busy? How long have you been up?"

"Please, May, the coffee?"

"Alright, I'm going, but are you sure I -"

"No, really, I'm better doing this myself. Just go and make the coffee, OK?"

With a shrug, May shuffled off to the kitchen. In edgy silence, Lizzie watched her go, until she had closed the door behind her. Then, with May safely out of the way, Lizzie redoubled her efforts to find somewhere to hide the letter. She went from room to room and back again, but nowhere looked safe enough. It had to be so ingenious a place that Lowry would not discover it. And Lizzie didn't want May finding it accidentally and reading it unnecessarily. But if Michael silenced Lizzie, then May would have to be warned about him, so it had to be possible for her to find it, should the need arise. Lizzie thought of slipping it inside one of the books in Father's study but, if anything were to happen to her, the letter would probably never be found: it was too difficult for May to negotiate the cluttered room, so she hardly ever went in there. Similarly, if Lizzie hid it upstairs, May would be unable to get up there to find it.

May called from the kitchen.

"Coffee's ready."

"Alright." Lizzie snapped, annoyed that May had been occupied for so little time. "I'll be there in a minute."

"Are you in the parlour?" asked May, apparently oblivious to the annoyance she was causing Lizzie, "I'll bring it through to you there, dear."

Almost at once, May appeared in the hall, carrying the small tray.

"Could you help me with this, dear?" she asked.

Barely hiding her irritation, Lizzie stuffed the letter into the waistband of her skirt then turned and snatched the tray from May's hands. She walked briskly into the parlour and in her haste upset the coffee pot, spilling some of the hot liquid onto her hand.

"Damn it!" she cried, more in anger at her own clumsiness than in pain.

May was concerned,

"Whatever's happened? Oh dear, your poor hand. Shall I get a damp cloth?"

"No," Lizzie winced, "just leave me alone."

Lizzie's patience with her sister was stretched near to breaking. Lack of sleep coupled with her anxiety over Lowry now threatened to rip it apart completely. She pulled her arm away from May and sat down at the table, the letter at her waist folding stiffly as she bent. She pulled it out and, for the want of somewhere better to put it, slid it under the edge of the tablecloth. May had seen nothing. She remained standing in the doorway, uncertain what to do.

"Are you going to sit down or not?" Lizzie snapped angrily.

May hurried over and sat down at once. Lizzie poured out the coffee and slid a cup towards her. May acknowledged it, with a brief nod of thanks, but said nothing and instead began to turn the cup around in its saucer as she tried to decide how best to open the conversation. The turning made a grinding noise that seemed immensely harsh in the silence of the room. Lizzie shot her a disapproving look but, deep in thought, May missed it entirely. After scraping the cup through another revolution, she decided to come straight out with it.

"Lizzie?"

"What?" asked Lizzie sharply.

"I have a confession to make."

Now it was Lizzie's turn to be baffled.

"What are you talking about?" she said, curious now, her voice no longer so sharp.

109

"It was me."

"What was?"

"Me. I lost the back door key. That's what you've been looking for, isn't it? I'm so sorry."

This was so unexpected that Lizzie nearly laughed out loud.

"Oh, you goose! No, I wasn't looking for the key. Don't worry about it. It'll turn up."

May was hugely relieved by this relaxed response, but also disconcerted. 'Relaxed' wasn't a word she would normally have associated with her sister. Lizzie's behaviour this morning was bewilderingly out of character. She hadn't even asked May how she had come to lose the key.

"Lizzie?"

'What now?' Lizzie wondered. Was May going to make another confession?

The pleasurable feeling of power that Lizzie had enjoyed when they had last argued began to stir again. May had apologised for losing the key. How bizarre was that! Lizzie had no intention of disabusing her; she would find the right moment to tell May she had the key safely hidden. But she would savour May's embarrassment a while longer. The anxious frown on May's face served only to heighten Lizzie's enjoyment of the moment. She continued to smile encouragement to May.

"Mmm?" she prompted.

"I was just wondering," May ventured, "how do you feel after yesterday, after your fall?" she hesitated, "Does your head still hurt?"

"A little. Why do you ask?"

"Oh no reason really. I was just wondering. You must have taken quite a knock."

"And?"

"Oh, nothing, dear. It's just that I believe that knocks

to the head can leave you feeling a little..."

"A little...?"

"Not quite yourself, dear."

"Oh I see," said Lizzie highly amused at May's discomfiture, "so you think I've gone a bit strange, a bit funny in the head, do you May? A bit mad perhaps?"

May managed a nervous laugh.

"No, dear, of course not. I just, you know, wondered if your head hurt, or anything."

"Well thank you for asking. As I said, yes, it does hurt a little, but don't worry, I'll take an aspirin. I'll be fine."

May smiled uncomfortably. Inside, she felt a deepening unease.

They finished their coffee in silence. Then, breakfast over, Lizzie announced that she had to go to town.

"But," said May in shocked amazement, "you only go to town on Mondays and Fridays."

May was looking very concerned now. This was very odd behaviour.

"Don't you think you should rest today, after yesterday's excitement?"

"Surely I can go to town whenever I please?" said Lizzie, her tone almost playful, teasing.

"I just thought that, after your fall, it might not be a good idea. Please stay home with me today. I can look after you."

"You, look after me?" Lizzie snorted, the humour in her voice evaporating, "I think we all know that's never going to happen."

"You all know? Who? Who knows?"

"It's just an expression, May. It's how people talk these days. But you wouldn't know about that, would you?"

Perhaps as a result of her exhaustion, Lizzie sensed the normal constraints of politeness falling away such that she felt nothing for May's feelings. She continued, with a cruel edge to her voice.

"No, May wouldn't know anything because May lives in an air-tight bubble, in her little comfort zone."

May looked at her in baffled incomprehension. Lizzie continued.

"Yes, May lives here in a time warp, while the world outside just passes her by." she said, warming to her topic, "Let me demonstrate. May, any idea what WMDs are? No? No idea at all? What a surprise! Know what Rap is? AIDS? Have you even the slightest idea what someone would mean if they told you to 'Chill out'? Didn't think so. Who was Ronald Reagan? Alice Cooper?"

May didn't know what to say. Lizzie was babbling, talking nonsense. It must be because of the fall. She must have banged her head very hard.

"Lizzie dear," she asked, speaking carefully, as if trying to attract the attention of an unpredictable child, "do you think it would be a good idea to go back to the hospital today, just for a check-up?"

"For all you know that might be just where I am going. You didn't ask me did you?"

May looked more hopeful.

"Well, are you?"

"Am I what?" Lizzie asked with artful innocence.

"Are you going to the hospital?"

"Let me think."

There followed an extravagant pause for contemplation before Lizzie continued.

"No. I have more important things to do. First, I have to go to the hardware store to buy some new locks."

May bit her lip.

"Can't that wait until you're feeling better? I'm really sorry about the key, but we don't have to get a replacement today, do we? Can't it wait till next week? Please."

"I'm buying new locks for all the doors," said Lizzie decisively, "Not just the one you lost."

May was downcast. She was wretched. It was her fault that Lizzie was having to go out today when she should really be resting quietly at home. May had caused all this upset by being selfish and thoughtless, in wanting to go out to watch her moths. Lizzie had told her not to, had made her promise, but May had broken that promise and now she wished, with all her heart, that she'd kept to her word. Then she wouldn't have lost the key. Now Lizzie was telling her that she'd wanted to replace all the locks anyway, but May was sure that Lizzie was only saying this to spare her feelings; not wanting her to feel guilty for losing the back door key.

She was in the hall, watching Lizzie ready herself to leave. Lizzie was wearing the same clothes as yesterday, still muddy from her fall, as if she had slept in them. There was a tear in one of the sleeves and a small patch of dried blood on one of her shoes. But, to May's astonishment, Lizzie seemed not to have noticed.

"Don't you think you should get changed before you go out, dear?"

Lizzie frowned at herself in the mirror but seemed at first not to see anything amiss in her appearance.

"The sleeve," May prompted, "and the mud on your skirt."

Lizzie half-turned, the better to see the mud on the back of her skirt.

"And your shoes, dear." said May.

Lizzie looked down and finally appeared to understand what May was talking about.

"I'll get changed." she said disinterestedly.

As Lizzie made her way upstairs, May collapsed into a chair. She was emotionally exhausted. There was something very wrong with Lizzie and May was frightened.

If only her legs weren't so useless. If only she could go to town instead of Lizzie. But she could not. All she could do was hope that Lizzie would come home safely and then allow May to care for her until she was feeling more like her old self.

Lizzie came down the stairs. She had changed her clothes but there was still something out of the ordinary about her, something that May could not define. Some intangible shift had taken place in Lizzie's character lately and May was unnerved by the change.

"Take care of yourself." she urged.

Lizzie was still angry.

"Well, that's a turn around isn't it?" she snapped, "It's usually my job to tell you to take care and then, of course, it's yours to completely ignore that advice. That's the way it's supposed to work, isn't it?"

May smiled weakly.

"Cat got your tongue?" Lizzie shrugged, "Don't worry, I'll be back soon"

Lizzie had no idea why she was talking like this and acting in this off-hand manner. With a detached part of herself she could see that she was disturbing May, but she couldn't stop the words coming. Perhaps May was right and the fall had affected her. Or again, could it be that the injury simply gave her licence to say all the things that had been left unsaid, building up into a mountain of resentment over the years? Was she merely using the fall as an excuse to say whatever she liked? She recognised this as a clear possibility but felt absolutely no remorse about it. Oddly, another compartment of her mind looked at this lack of remorse and was pleasantly surprised by it. Lizzie was aware of watching and analysing herself, over and over, in ever greater detail.

"Hogwash!" she said out loud, a random word to dismiss her busy thoughts. She had to focus. She had work to do.

"Did you say, 'Hogwash', dear?" Poor May was still struggling to understand what was going on.

"Just an expression," Lizzie grunted, as she pulled on her coat. She smiled, unable to resist another tease. "It's used all the time these days. But now it means something like OK, or 'I'm ready', or 'Everything's OK', as in 'Everything's going Hogwash.' Do you see?"

"Yes, I see. Thank you dear. I'll try to remember," said May, pathetically eager to please.

'Gosh!' the detached part of Lizzie's brain marvelled, 'Still no guilt. Quite, quite amazing!'

Worried though she was for her sister, May was still hugely relieved when the door finally closed behind Lizzie and there was peace. She found herself shaking. What was this? Fear? Good Lord, yes, fear. But fear of what? Not of Lizzie. Lizzie was acting strangely, certainly, but Lizzie would never do anything to harm her. Never. Maybe this feeling wasn't fear then. Whatever it was, it was powerful; May was still shaking. She gripped her cane tightly with one hand and reached out to steady herself against the wall with the other. Even her arm was shaking.

A roaring wave began in her ears. She swallowed hard, then blinked in a vain effort to clear her vision. With the wobbliness in her legs worsening, she struggled along the corridor, leaning more and more on the wall for support. When she finally reached her room, it was all she could do to take the two or three steps inside before she fainted, thankfully falling onto the welcoming safety of the bed.

After a few moments, May began to swim up, out of

the silence, to consciousness. The roaring in her ears returned and then gave way to a high-pitched whine that filled her head. She felt nauseous but fought against the urge by clamping her mouth shut and swallowing repeatedly. Eventually her world stopped turning. She was back. But she was exhausted. Promising herself that she would take just a few minutes of rest, she shut her eyes and fell, almost instantly, into a deep sleep.

Lizzie was walking along the lane. Unlike her usual purposeful marching, she was meandering quite slowly. Her mind was similarly wandering. She was still intoxicated by the sense of freedom and power she had again felt. That inhibitions had faded away and allowed her to feel no compunction in tormenting her sister was quite extraordinary. It was as if she was detached from her normal sense of right and wrong: detached from her normal sense of self.

    At this thought, Lizzie suddenly felt an emptiness open up within her. What was the matter with her? How could she act like this towards May? How could she take any pleasure in a game of cat and mouse which poor May had no chance of winning? Consumed with her self-analysis and frightened by the change she saw in her own personality, Lizzie could not for the moment remember what she was doing out here in the lane. Indeed she was only marginally aware of her surroundings. Her mind was in turmoil.

    Muttering quietly to herself, she began to run through the list of things she had to do. First, to the bank to take out some money. Then to Billy's store, to get the locks for the doors. Better get them for all the windows too. How many locks altogether? Let's see, two doors and, two, three, five...heavens, nine windows on the ground floor alone. And two, four, six (seven, if you count the tiny one in the bathroom) upstairs. That was going to be expensive. Better go to the bank and get some more money out. Then what? Oh yes, then to Billy's. How many locks was that again?

The repeating of the list of tasks was perhaps a subconscious attempt to impose some order. To an observer Lizzie would have appeared self-absorbed, perhaps mildly confused, but no more so than was the stereotypical norm for an elderly lady. No one would have given her a second glance. The hollowness she felt and the turmoil of fear and confusion raging inside her head were hidden from the world. She had to keep that turmoil from coming to the surface. She had to concentrate. What was she doing out here?

Then it came to her, as it had yesterday, in a rush of images: the man in the garden; a knife in her own hand; May's frightened face at the window; the hospital; that man sitting in their kitchen, so foreign in those familiar cosy surroundings and his pale, grey eyes searching hers, probing. Probing for what? What did he want? What was his game?

Thinking of the man, she was immediately aware of where she was: ambling along the track into town, oblivious to the dangers that could be lurking there. The realisation that she had been so completely ignoring all the precautions that would normally have been second nature to her, filled her with terrible foreboding. What was the matter with her? What was happening? She roughly wiped away the tears that were starting to sting at her eyes.

She was alert now, looking from side to side and glancing behind her. There was no one in sight. Good. She drew herself up, straightened her back and walked on with renewed purpose and determination.

Little Danny Smith was, as usual, swinging on the fence of

the school yard.

"Miss Oatley?" he called out, "Look!"

Miss Oatley pocketed a confiscated pack of gum and, having gently shooed away the half-indignant, half-resigned complaints of its previous owner, walked over to Danny.

"What is it Daniel?" she asked in her gentle, sugary voice.

Taking his hand in hers, their palms closed and Miss Oatley felt something that should not have been there. With some reluctance, she eased her hand away, to see what the offending something was. She was vaguely aware that Danny hadn't answered her.

"What have you seen?" she prompted automatically, all the while concentrating on whatever it was on Danny's palm. Ah, thank goodness, it was just a glob of mud. Mystery solved, she returned her attention to the boy.

"Well Daniel?"

"Look." he replied, unhelpfully.

Miss Oatley scanned the road, a tiny puzzled frown above her nose. Nothing seemed out of the ordinary.

"What is it?" she asked, her tone becoming slightly brittle, "What am I supposed to be looking for?"

"Look," said Danny, pointing with a stubby finger, "The falling down lady."

Miss Oatley's pretty smile froze as she stared across at Lizzie. The frown deepened. Surely this formidable lady couldn't be the irritating old crone from yesterday. Good God, it was! The frown becoming a scowl, Miss Oatley grabbed Danny's hand and roughly pulled him away from the fence.

"Stop wasting my time." she snapped, her face colouring at the memory of yesterday's wasted effort and at the dreadful way in which that paramedic had spoken to her. Such rudeness! She marched back across the school yard, carving an instant path through the jostling children and forgetting that she still had Danny's hand in hers. Being dragged onwards and half-skipping in an effort to keep up with her, he bounced along at her heels like a cart-wheeling puppy.

When Lizzie arrived, somewhat breathless, at Billy Pierce's hardware store, she stopped for a moment to catch her breath then marched in, straight to the counter. A nondescript young woman was at the till, reading a glossy magazine.
"Can I help you?" she mumbled, without looking up.
"Yes," said Lizzie imperiously, "kindly tell Mr Pierce that I am here."
Now she had the girl's attention.
"Uuh?" she said, looking up from her magazine and frowning.
Faced with the girl's blank expression, Lizzie found herself visualising a large question mark in a bubble above the girl's head, just like in the cartoon strips in the Funnies section of the newspapers.
"Go and tell Mr Pierce that I am here." she repeated, slowly.
"Sorry?"
Lizzie was beginning to think that the girl must be a bit simple. She decided to establish some facts.
"Is he here?"
"Who? Mr Pierce?"
In Lizzie's mind's eye the question mark over this dim-witted girl's head was now neon. And it was flashing.
"Yes." said Lizzie, now with exaggerated slowness, "Mr Pierce. Is he here?"
"Well, yeah."
"Then go and tell him and quickly please. I don't have all day."

"But-" the girl began, only to stop abruptly, intimidated by Lizzie's ominously raised eyebrow. OK, OK. She had no idea who this woman was, but that wasn't her problem. The customer was always right and if the customer wanted to speak to the boss so much, then let him sort it out. Without another word to Lizzie, the girl slapped her magazine shut and left, through the door behind the counter.

Lizzie heard the girl climbing the stairs to a room above the shop. Then muffled voices and more footsteps on the stairs. She made out Billy's voice.

"You didn't get her name? Well, what does she look like?"

And then the girl.

"I dunno...old?"

"Shhh, for goodness sake, Jo."

Piqued, Lizzie endeavoured to make herself look slightly less old before Billy and the girl appeared: she straightened her back and raised her head to tighten the slack skin of her neck. The door opened and Jo came out first, waving vaguely in Lizzie's direction.

Billy's face was a picture.

"Lizzie? Lizzie Atwell?" he gawped, "Is it you?"

Lizzie's answer was brusque.

"Don't be ridiculous, Billy, of course it's me."

Jo sniggered. Billy picked her magazine from the counter and used it to shoo her away.

"Go check the last delivery. It's in the storeroom."

Jo grabbed the magazine from his hand and hurried away, happily anticipating at least a half hour's uninterrupted reading. Billy watched her go.

"My daughter." he muttered, apologetically, nodding after her, "Image of her mother."

There was embarrassment rather then parental pride in his voice. He pulled a chair over to the counter and gestured to Lizzie to sit. She sat down, grateful to rest her legs, after the final furious pace of her walk into town. Once settled, she got directly to the business in hand.

"Locks. I need locks. Do you sell them?"

She made a cursory look around the shop, though she had not the slightest intention of going hunting for the items herself. Abreast of current affairs she may be and familiar with the latest nonsense in youth culture, but Lizzie was a firm believer in the art of shopping in the old fashioned way. She liked to be waited on, by knowledgeable and respectful staff.

Billy stared across at Lizzie. He knew her of old, but he couldn't recall her ever having come into his shop before today. He would sometimes see her passing by, across the street on Mondays or Fridays, but he hadn't actually spoken to her since her poor mother's funeral, years ago. Looking at her now, Billy was amazed at how old her face had become, especially around the eyes; however, in other ways, she was still easily recognisable as that tearaway girl in the oak tree gang. She was as thin as ever and her hair was still frizzy, albeit slightly more controlled than he remembered from their childhood. All in all, Lizzie was much the same as she had been then. And not just in looks. Judging by her performance here in the shop, she still carried herself with the dignity, bordering on arrogance, that she had always displayed. It was a dignity born of being Frank's sister, the first, indeed for a long time, the only girl in the gang: unique.

Lizzie had had enough of Billy's staring.

"Well? Do you sell them or not?"

"Locks? Yes, of course, all sorts. What do you need?"

Lizzie asked for two door locks, the strongest that he had, and sixteen window locks, again the strongest that he had. Billy frowned.

"If you don't mind me asking, Lizzie, why do you need

so many?"

"And, if I do mind?" Lizzie asked in her haughtiest tone.

Billy shrugged apologetically.

"I know it's none of my business, but it seems like a lot of locks all at once, that's all."

Looking up at Billy's big, honest face, Lizzie immediately regretted her sharpness. He was such a simple soul, with such an open, childlike face that it was practically impossible to be unkind to him. Being the cause of any hurt in those big, blue eyes of his, brought on such remorse that the offender suffered at least as much as did Billy. It had always been that way. It was part of what made Billy special.

"Forgive me, Billy." said Lizzie, relaxing a little, "It's been a difficult week and I'm perhaps a little over tired. We've had problems with a prowler, so I need locks to replace the old ones we've got, with the latest models."

Billy was shocked. He leant forward solicitously, his face close to hers.

"A prowler? Dear Lord, are you and your sister alright?"

Lizzie straightened again, moving away slightly.

She felt she had to be careful with Billy. He had always been very attentive towards her and, when they were both young, it had been acknowledged by everyone that he was infatuated with her. Acknowledged by everyone, that is, except Lizzie. She had recognised his interest in her, it would have been impossible not to, but she had refused even to let herself consider that he might feel anything as deep as love for her. Billy was sweet-natured, but he was too pliant. Too weak. Lizzie had wanted, and she thought deserved, something more: someone exceptional. Someone like Frank. But of course, even had her duties at home allowed, there had never been anyone who met, or even came close to that standard. Waiting for the perfect man who never was, Lizzie had always taken great care not to encourage Billy in any way. But, despite her care, she had suffered seeing disappointment in those big, sorrowful eyes many times. It had been difficult, but it had to be done.

Now, here in his shop, she felt the need for that old wariness return, in the face of Billy's evident desire to comfort her. She put up the same defences she always had and answered him curtly.

"We're managing, thank you. Now, could I have those locks?"

Billy felt her guard slamming into place. That same wall had gone up whenever he had tried to be anything more than a friend to her. And he had tried, so many times. Lizzie was the only woman that he had ever longed for and even now she still held a fascination for him. From the start, she had set herself apart from the rest of the gang, supremely proud that she was Frank's favourite. She was older than Billy; an object of awe to all the younger boys. She was a fearless, skinny, wild-haired tomboy, in baggy dungarees, who nevertheless insisted on being treated like a grand lady. To Billy her self-imposed remoteness was alluring and, to his eyes, her hair was a wonderful explosion, her oversized clothes and her thin frame, endearing.

The lovesick youth had hoped to impress her. He had shared with her his dreams of learning to fly and travelling the world. He'd never known whether she had been impressed, but at least she hadn't laughed, as many others had, when he came back to town having failed to pass the entry tests to train to be a pilot. That failure was the biggest regret of Billy's life, but it was regret heightened by the knowledge that he had failed to achieve something worthy of Lizzie Atwell's admiration.

And time had repeated itself.

He was nearly an old man himself now and, looking around at the crowded shelves, the special offers, the end of line 'bargains' and the unsold impulse orders, Billy felt suddenly embarrassed, not only by his own decline into middle age, but also by the somewhat down at heel clutter of his store. There was nothing to impress here. Certainly nothing to impress a woman like Lizzie.

Nothing had changed.

"Billy!" Lizzie's tone was sharp. It snapped him out of his day dream.

"Locks." he said, "Yes I'll get them for you. Eighteen was it?"

Lizzie felt more comfortable now that Billy had stopped gawping at her and gone away to get the locks. She settled back in her chair and waited. After much rummaging around, Billy gathered all her purchases together on the counter and rang up their prices on the till. Eighteen locks made for quite a heavy weight and Billy wasn't sure that his store's brown paper bags would be up to the job.

"These are very heavy. I tell you what. Why don't I bring them around for you later?"

"No, thank you Billy, there's no need." said Lizzie, quickly heading off an unwanted visit. "Here, let me pay you."

Lizzie handed the money to Billy, who accepted it and returned her change thoughtfully.

"They really are very heavy." he said, sounding worried. "Here, just you try to lift this."

Billy raised the bag a few inches off the counter and proffered it to Lizzie but she didn't take it; she didn't need to. It was clear from the strain on Billy's face that the bag would be far too heavy for her to carry for even a short distance. She bit her lip and Billy hoped that her silence meant she accepted the good sense in what he was saying.

With a noisy slamming of doors, Jo returned from the storeroom. She stopped and looked from her father to Lizzie, uneasy, sensing the tension between them. Billy glanced at Jo then back to Lizzie. He'd thought of something else.

"Who are you going to get to put the locks in for you?"

Lizzie hadn't even considered that as yet.

"Could you recommend someone?"

Billy considered.

"I reckon Steve. Steven Owens. He helps me out here in the store. He's a good kid, very reliable".

Lizzie saw her way out. She stood up.

"Very well then," she said briskly, snapping her handbag shut, "please give the locks to Mr Owens and have him come fit them tomorrow morning, but not before eleven. I leave it to you to suggest to him what he should charge. I trust your judgement. Thank you. Good day Billy."

Lizzie added the merest nod of acknowledgement towards Jo then turned and left the shop as quickly as possible.

Billy stood at the counter, gazing hopelessly after Lizzie as she walked out of his shop. Standing next to her father, Jo looked up and saw the devotion animating his face. She followed his gaze, stunned to realise that the object of this desire was the old woman. She was appalled.

"That's gross! No wonder Mum left. Do you look at all the old women like that?"

Billy turned to her and, for a second, Jo was stunned into silence. She had never seen him so coldly angry. He spoke slowly and deliberately, through clenched teeth.

"Be quiet, you stupid, stupid girl. You have no idea

what you're talking about. And I don't ever want to hear you talk about her like that again."

Recklessly defiant, Jo threw back her head and laughed at him.

"God you're pathetic! I saw how you were looking at her! And I saw how the old cow treated you. You're nothing to her. Can't you see that?"

Billy's anger was spent. He looked down at his daughter with resigned distaste. It could have been Sue, her mother, talking. She'd called him pathetic and worse. Their arguments had been bitter, and Jo's birth had not brought them back together as he'd hoped it would. Sue used to say she felt trapped. She hated her life and she despised him. Finally she left him, saying that she was going to get a life for herself; she wasn't going to stay on in a dead-end town with a dead-end man. And now here was Jo mouthing the same words as her mother and with the same overt contempt.

The worst of it, the hardest to bear, was the fact that they were both right. He was pathetic. He was a dead-end man. His ex-wife and now his daughter had seen through the threadbare veneer he displayed to the world. They had seen the pitiful, useless man within and they despised him for his weakness.

Disgusted with himself, his anger burst back into flame. He grabbed Jo's arm and pushed her away.

"Leave me alone!" he almost shouted, "Leave me alone!"

Jo fell back against the counter and watched, her face a petulant glare of resentment, as Billy stomped back upstairs. It served him right, she thought, that the old hag had given him the cold shoulder. Still rubbing her bruised elbow, Jo smiled, pleased at the way she had handled her father. She had managed to provoke what was, for him, a rare outburst of emotion. He'd even shouted. He had finally shown some fire and it was her goading that had stoked the flames. It was just a shame that it had taken that bossy, dried up old woman to light the embers in the first place. A shame the dopey old fool had obviously saved all the passion in his life for that old witch.

Pathetic!

11

May awoke, initially confused at finding herself on her bed; but fully dressed. Slowly, a collection of disturbing images began to drift back: Lizzie's strange behaviour, her torn and dirty clothes and her going into town. Was she back yet? May strained to listen, half in dread, half in hope. But no, the house was completely still and silent but for the clock in the hall faithfully marking time. And that was strange. May couldn't usually hear that heartbeat of the house from here. She must have left her door open when she came to bed. Why had she done that?

With that question the memory of her fainting came back to her. Remembering her struggle to get from the hall, along the corridor, to the door of her room, she was deeply shaken to realise just how very fortunate she had been to reach the safety of the bed; when she could so easily have crashed to the floor, unconscious. May shuddered involuntarily at the thought.

For years now, the stiffness in her legs had made walking arduous and slow, constantly irritating and occasionally painful. But, if she were to fall and break any of her brittle old bones, she knew she might well spend the rest of her days in a wheelchair. That prospect had long been a secret fear, the dread of which kept her from ever testing the limits of her self-imposed containment within the house and garden. Familiar with every tree, every shrub and every tussock of grass, she could have navigated a safe path through the garden blindfolded. Lizzie did nothing in the garden. It was May's domain and what, to an outsider, would have seemed severely limited horizons was, to May, a world of freedom especially when compared to the prospect of forever being trapped within a machine, however benign its purpose. Lying on her bed now, she gave silent thanks to Fate for sparing her this time. Her gratitude was heart-felt and her sense of relief profound; but she felt drained, hollowed out, empty. And this wasn't the first time May had fainted. She supposed she had a problem with her blood but she had put off seeking medical help. Maybe the time was coming when she would have to get Lizzie to arrange for the doctor to come see her. May simply couldn't risk a damaging fall.

She was exhausted. Closing her eyes, she felt the tingle on her face as a single tear slipped down the soft folds of her cheek, into her ear. It pooled there for a second, tickling, then dropped, with a gentle pat, onto the linen pillowcase below. Her breathing was calm and deep.

She lay still for a long time, recovering, until finally she decided she must try to get up. Slowly, she eased her legs to the side of the bed and lowered her feet to the floor. Then, thin fingers gripping the headboard for support, she drew herself up to a sitting position and held her breath for a second, before sighing with a broad smile of relief: her head was clear. There was no dizziness. The crisis was over. It was over and she had come through. And she was thirsty she realised. She wanted a strong cup of coffee. With that refreshing goal firmly in mind, she straightened her cardigan and smoothed her skirt, reached for her stick and cautiously rose to her feet.

It took May some time to reach the kitchen. She

opened the door and scanned the room. Where was the coffee pot? Where were the cups? For a moment she frowned, having again forgotten that she had not just woken from a night's sleep. She was set in her normal morning routine, but it soon came back to her that she had already eaten breakfast with Lizzie, just a few hours ago…in the parlour. Of course, the breakfast things would still be there. Sure enough, the cups, plates and coffee pot were just as they had left them, on the table in the parlour.

May stacked the plates and carried them carefully to the kitchen. Returning to collect the remainder, she lifted the empty coffee pot and automatically smoothed the tablecloth beneath it with her hand. She stopped. There was something there, under the cloth. Setting the coffee pot down, she heaved back the corner of the tablecloth, revealing the sealed envelope containing Lizzie's letter. May stopped, looking down at it, a frown deepening on her forehead. She blinked the water from her eyes. Her own name was clearly written on the front of the envelope, in what was unmistakably Lizzie's looping handwriting.

May was completely taken aback, a comical statue, frozen in the action of lifting the heavy cloth, a look of complete bafflement on her face. Struggling to reason a way through her confusion, she tried to imagine why on earth Lizzie would have written her a letter. It could be a card, she supposed. But her birthday was not for months and, more to the point, this was Lizzie and Lizzie never sent cards: didn't believe in them. Only last Christmas, Lizzie had described the entire greeting card industry as, 'The canny and profitable manipulation of the emotional and gullible by the avaricious and cynical'. Lizzie said she thought she'd read it somewhere and May had been so amused that she committed it to memory herself.

Recalling it now, she smiled again, in spite of herself. Lizzie rarely used such long words, being a woman of actions rather than fancy talk, but the sentiment behind them was so very typical of her: opinionated, unsentimental and direct.

But if not a birthday card, what? Fascinated, May now turned her mind to other possibilities.

Maybe the letter was an apology from Lizzie for her bizarre behaviour this morning. But again no: Lizzie insisted on always being in the right. Admitting fault and apologising for it had never come easily to her. Certainly she wouldn't readily commit an apology to paper in a permanent record. Also, from the purely logistical perspective, Lizzie wouldn't have had time in which to write an apology, or anything else for that matter, before heading off to town. No, the letter, if letter it was, must have been written before, perhaps long before, they'd sat down to breakfast this morning.

With mounting anxiety, May pictured Lizzie carrying the letter around for days or even weeks, unable to bring herself to hand it over. Perhaps Lizzie had something so awful to say that she simply couldn't say it in person. Was she ill? Had she been given some terrible news at the hospital? Was she dying? Good Lord! What if this was Lizzie's Will?

A cold apprehension settled on May. She made no move to pick up the letter. Paralysed by indecision, she was torn: desperate to read it, but also in dread of what she might discover if she did. What to do? In another moment she had made her decision. She released the cloth and let it fall back into place, concealing the envelope once again. Lizzie had not yet felt able to give it to her, perhaps she never would, so it was not for May to take and read it. May's respect for her sister was such that she was prepared to wait indefinitely, saying nothing about it, until Lizzie was ready to give the letter to her.

May stroked the cloth, smoothing it over the hidden letter. She nodded. This was the right thing to do. She picked up the coffee pot and shuffled out of the room.

She was soon sitting in the kitchen sipping her coffee. For a short while, the hidden letter had pushed everything else from her thoughts, but her earlier collapse had now come back to her and again she thanked her stars that she hadn't suffered serious harm. If she had broken a bone in a fall, she might have been lying there even now, perhaps conscious but unable to move or call for help. And, worst of all, she would have been completely alone. Today, of all days, when May really needed her, Lizzie had insisted on going into town and leaving her all alone. And on top of everything else there was a prowler in the neighbourhood.

May was rarely prey to prolonged self-pity or to such feelings of helplessness, because she had her gift for discarding and then almost completely dismissing any unpleasantness. But now, sitting alone at the kitchen table, fully realising how narrowly she had escaped injury, May felt absolutely miserable. Her eyes, always weepy, now began to overflow. She sniffled noisily and felt for her handkerchief in her sleeve. It wasn't there. Darn it! Why is it that nothing is where it should be when you need it? Rising stiffly to her feet, she went to pull a sheet of paper towel from its roll by the sink. She blinked and patted at her eyes, her vision gradually becoming less fluid. Beyond the window, what had previously appeared to be as molten as sea-weeds, undulating with the swirling films in her eyes, slowly firmed into solid trees and bushes. Drifting, sparkling stars and rippling splashes of light faded away and, when her sight finally cleared, the garden re-emerged, bathed evenly in sunlight; the scene finally at rest.

Only one movement remained and it caught May's attention. She frowned. It was a large black cat, creeping low across the lawn, its belly brushing the ground. May leaned forward in an attempt to see what prey he was stalking. She could see nothing. But, reaching to tap on the window she became convinced, all at once, that the cat must be stalking the wonderful Polyphemus. In sudden panic, May found herself moving towards the back door, determined that she would rescue the moth and put it up somewhere high where no cats could get at it. How she was going to climb up to such a safe, high spot had not yet occurred to her. Also overlooked was the missing backdoor key. May's hand went automatically up to the usual place on the wall and felt nothing but the empty hook. In the same instant, she remembered the loss of the key. Giving way to anger, she furiously rattled the door handle. She knew that such a display of temper would achieve absolutely nothing but, had her legs not been so stiff, she would probably also have kicked the door for good measure.

May snatched up her stick and, furious at her own slowness, hurried as best she could to the front door. But, as soon as she reached it, before she had even grasped at the latch, the door opened and Lizzie, stopped in mid-stride, stood gaping at her.

"Have you been standing here, just waiting for me again?" Lizzie demanded, startled.

"Of course not. Don't be silly."

May was about to tell Lizzie that she was on her way out to rescue the moth, but then she realised that her having to use the front door would remind Lizzie of the lost backdoor key. It was better not to bring up all that unpleasantness again.

May noticed a poker that hung heavily from Lizzie's hand. She frowned. Surely Lizzie hadn't armed herself with that just to go shopping. Had Lizzie been carrying it around the town, from shop to shop? That surely wasn't normal behaviour. The outside world couldn't have changed as much as that.

Lizzie followed May's worried gaze.

"Yes, isn't that lucky?" she said, "I found it at the corner on my way back from the shops. It had rolled to the edge of the path."

'Nonsense' thought May, 'that's our old poker. We've had it years. Why on earth is she lying like this?' But out loud she simply said,

"You look tired, dear. Come on in. Shall I make you a camomile tea?"

May stepped back to allow Lizzie to come in, then followed her to the kitchen.

Lizzie was exhausted from the brisk march to and from Billy's store. She brushed aside May's worried look, but accepted the offer of the tea and took her seat at the kitchen table.

"I'll have the tea and then I think I'll go for a lie down." she said, closing her eyes, "It's been a long morning."

May busied herself making the tea, all the while snatching sidelong glances at Lizzie who was now resting her head on her folded hands. She was obviously exhausted. Was she ill?

"Yes, dear, you do that. You must be tired out." May agreed sympathetically.

She had tried to convey her sincere concern in the tone of her voice, fervently hoping that Lizzie would sense it, feel reassured and perhaps feel able at last to confide in her. Surely Lizzie must see that there was no need to hide her news, however bad it might be?

Whatever it was that she'd so far only been able to put in writing, should now be said face to face. May couldn't help but wonder if Lizzie's obvious tiredness was something to do with whatever she had divulged in her letter, a symptom of an illness perhaps? What was the problem? Both May's longing to know what was in the letter and her fierce love for her sister, were evident on her face. Lizzie looked up, noticed May's intense, meaning-laden stare and instantly resented the attention.

"What are you looking at? If you've got something to say then say it. Don't just stand there staring like an idiot."

Surprised at Lizzie's abrupt reaction, May averted her eyes. She thought for a moment. Patience would be needed if she were to encourage Lizzie to be open with her. So, forcing herself to disregard Lizzie's rudeness, she instead focused on the loneliness and apprehension that Lizzie must be enduring.

"Lizzie, dear, I was wondering if there was anything you'd like to talk about, anything you'd like to say." she hazarded.

"Like what?"

"Oh, I don't know, anything you might want to get off your chest." said May in the most encouraging of tones.

Lizzie's face darkened and May knew at once that she had mishandled the situation.

"You've got a nerve!" Lizzie snapped, "You're expecting an apology from me aren't you?"

"What? No, I -."

"Well you can forget that. If anyone's owed an apology around here, it's me; I've just had to go all the way into town to get new locks. I'm absolutely exhausted. What on earth makes you think that I owe **you** an apology? How dare you even think it?"

"No Lizzie, you've got it wrong, I didn't think -"

"No. You never do. You're just a selfish, selfish woman. And I've had enough! Do you hear me? I have had enough!"

Lizzie rose to her feet and, ignoring May's attempts to persuade her to stay, strode out of the room. She stamped up the stairs and slammed the door of her room behind her.

Though May called up to her from time to time throughout the afternoon, Lizzie stayed in her room, sleeping intermittently, for many hours, only finally coming down for a sandwich late in the evening. The two women ate in stony silence and retired to their rooms with barely a 'Goodnight' spoken.

Lizzie did not have a good night. She had initially planned to remain fully dressed and alert, watching and listening, as she had last night, but tonight she had simply felt too debilitated. She undressed and climbed into her bed. But the fear that Michael Lowry, having read her police file, might break into the house to silence her, meant that, though bone-weary, Lizzie was unable to relax and surrender to sleep. After many anxious hours, she greeted the first paling of the sky with exhausted relief and allowed herself to doze off.

When her alarm clock leapt into life, less than an hour later, Lizzie's whole body jerked awake immediately. With eyes wide but unfocused, she swept her arms about in a furious effort to stop the deafening noise. She slammed her hand on the top of the clock. Silence. Blessed peace. Lizzie fell back into the pillows, her heart still racing. It took several minutes, lying in the ringing silence of the room, before her breathing was calm once more.

Although still weary, Lizzie's mind was now clear and she began to plan her day.

It was a Friday and, creature of habit that she was, she

would go to the shop as usual to buy food. The library would be open today, but Lizzie would have to forgo the reading of the newspapers because Steven, Billy's lock fitter, was due at eleven. Lizzie knew she would have to walk quite quickly but she could do it; she could be back in time. And she would feel so much safer once the locks were in place. She could hardly wait. Perhaps tonight she would feel secure enough to enjoy a good night's sleep. A restful night: that would be wonderful. Merely the thought of sleep had Lizzie's eyes slipping closed for one delicious second, before she realised what was happening. Lids snapped open again. She must stay awake. There wasn't time to go back to sleep now. This was going to be a busy day.

With a short, determined intake of breath, Lizzie sat up and dragged herself out of bed. She washed, splashing cold water on her face, then dressed and went downstairs. There was no sign of May. Lizzie tapped gently at her sister's door but heard only quiet snoring from within.

'Let her rest' she thought, 'I'll probably be back before she's even out of bed.'

Beneath her conscious thought was the understanding that it was probably less stressful for May to sleep through the periods when Lizzie was out of the house, rather than be awake and wandering the empty house alone. Anticipating May's needs, deciding what was best for her, was second nature to Lizzie; the habit of a lifetime, not easily discarded even in the face of her growing irritation at May's helplessness. She decided to let May sleep on.

Lizzie was just about to leave the house when it occurred to her that she hadn't said anything to May about the young man coming to fix the new locks today. She decided to write a quick note and leave it on the breakfast table where May would be sure to find it if she woke before Lizzie's return. Lizzie propped the hurriedly scribbled note up against the teapot, gathered up her bag and swept out of the house. Behind her, on the kitchen table lay the house keys, forgotten in her haste.

Some time later, May awoke with a start, sweating and hugely relieved to be free of a terrible nightmare. In it, as always in her dreams, she had been able to walk and even run; here her arthritis, an affliction of her everyday reality, never held her back. But, whereas usually she found herself skipping through the sunny afternoons and warm evenings of her youth, perhaps even flying through crystal moonlight with her beloved moths, this dream had her running to escape from something. This was running in blind panic, not skipping, not running free, but running scared. Something ill-defined, but terrible was chasing her, taking huge, thundering strides for every tiny step of her own. Howling darkness was racing up behind her, threatening to engulf her, but she just couldn't move fast enough to escape it. Her feet no longer seemed to impact on the ground beneath them. She was pushing with all her might but there was nothing to push against, no resistance. Frantic pounding of her legs and thrusts of her arms had no effect. She was an insect caught in clear, sticky amber, helpless in the path of the oncoming terror.

May woke just as she was about to be overwhelmed.

She lay still and, as the nightmare began to fade, she felt some strength gradually returning to her shaken body. It had been a dream, nothing to be afraid of. And, though it had been dreadful, it was over now. She was alright and she must now get on with the day.

After dressing, she went to the kitchen, looking for Lizzie. She found and read Lizzie's scribbled note. However, far from feeling reassured by Lizzie's thoughtfulness, May read her message as a warning. Lizzie had written, obviously in a great hurry, that a man would be coming to the house but May was not to worry because Lizzie would be back soon and she would 'deal with him'. Whatever did that mean? Obviously the man was the prowler, but how was Lizzie going to deal with him? What was her plan? And why had she left the house keys here with the note? What was May supposed to do with them?

In her note, Lizzie had neglected to say where she was going. As she always did some shopping on a Friday, she had simply assumed that May would realise where she was. But, in May's view, Lizzie had been acting very oddly lately and it didn't occur to her that Lizzie would be doing anything as normal and routine as the Friday shop.

May was now beset with worry as to where Lizzie might be and what she might be planning to do. Standing at the table, deep in thought, May dabbed at the water from her eyes and let her gaze absently wander the cluttered kitchen. There was the poker, still propped up against the kitchen chair as Lizzie had left it yesterday. If Lizzie had felt the need to take it with her into town yesterday, why on earth hadn't she taken it with her for protection today, when she knew the prowler was coming? It didn't make sense. Could Lizzie have left it for her to use? May picked up the poker and weighed it in her hand, but it made her arm ache. It was much too heavy for her to wield; she didn't have Lizzie's strength. No, it had been thoughtful of Lizzie to leave it for her but, if the prowler was coming back, May would have to find some other means of defending herself.

May thought hard, turning for inspiration first to the stirring yarns, with their feats of daring and implausible escapes from danger, that she had so enjoyed reading over the years. Not surprisingly, these melodramatic literary escapades suggested nothing that would be of any practical use to her in her current predicament. There were no knights on chargers or selfless heroes to come to her rescue, but the recollection of these wonderfully tall tales did at least give a lift to her spirits. May didn't feel quite so alone with all these old familiar friends in mind. She even managed a weak smile.

With reluctance, she pushed the novella heroics from her thoughts. She knew she had to think clearly. She had to concentrate.

Unable to walk quickly, flight was clearly not an option. All at once the nightmare with its terror of being unable to move, paralysed but fully conscious, sprang back into her mind. Her smile vanished and she shivered violently. It was vital that she find some means by which to protect herself.

After a few moments of intense concentration her face deepened into a frown. A solution had become clear to her, but it arose from some confusing and disturbing images from her past. Long buried memories stirred and came to the fore and for that moment May was focused on an awful event she'd hidden, even from herself, for decades. Something had happened all those years ago, something that shouldn't have happened: a terrible accident. The recollection was painful to confront, but at least May now knew that she could defend herself. She knew what she had to do.

She had, it seemed, done it once before.

The moment of recall passed and the memories sank back beneath May's conscious mind. As the spell of introspection waned, her face relaxed and her mood lifted. All unpleasantness forgotten, she was now content, retaining only the knowledge of how she was going to deal with the prowler. And her grim plan of action could sit quite comfortably alongside her now cheerful disposition, as she was no longer conscious of its associated memories. Her ability to file away and subsequently completely neglect life's disagreeable events had come to her aid once again.

But, first things first, she needed a nice cup of tea. She went to the sink to fill the kettle, a smile of anticipation forming on her lips.

Lizzie had raced to do her shopping. As usual, she was unhindered by any unnecessary conversation with people in the shops and today she strode right past the impressive, colonnaded entrance of the library, barely slowing her pace. Behind her, at the window, Miss Willets was startled. Surely that was the old lady who came in to read the papers? She peered closer to the window. It was. What on earth, Miss Willets wondered, could have happened to stop her coming in today? She'd come to the library, every Monday and every Friday that the library was open, without fail since...well, since before Miss Willets had been working here. Such was the predictability of Lizzie's normal habits that Miss Willets had already wheeled the newspaper rack over to Lizzie's customary table here, by the window. Watching Lizzie's hurried progress out of town, Miss Willets frowned, disconcerted, the old lady's unprecedented change in routine had left her observer quite unsettled.

Still walking briskly, Lizzie continued to make good time and was back home well before eleven. She climbed to the front door, looking around her as cautiously as ever whilst scrabbling in her handbag, feeling for the keys. Her brows knitted. Where were those keys? Not wanting to give all her attention to the search and risk being taken unawares by the prowler, Lizzie put down her shopping and transferred her handbag to her other hand. But she had no better luck searching with her right hand. In the end she had to snatch a quick glance down into the bag. No. All the other bits and pieces were there, including her purse, but the keys were definitely not. So where were they? Had someone snatched them from her handbag when she was in town? If so, why had they left her purse? That made no sense. Thank goodness she was having the locks changed. Her keys would be of no use to the pickpocket after that. Ha! Serve him right!

Lizzie tried knocking on the door but there was no response: May was at that moment preoccupied, deep in her unsettling memories and quite unaware of her surroundings. Lizzie's hand went to the backdoor key, safe on its ribbon about her neck. She could get in at the backdoor, but May mustn't see her using the key, or Lizzie would have some explaining to do. Cautiously, Lizzie began quietly to skirt around the side of the house, crouching low and making as little noise as possible.

In the kitchen, May had filled the kettle and was about to turn to the stove when she noticed a movement outside. To her delight, the moth was back again and it looked very much bigger, clumsily stumbling across the lawn. That horrible black cat hadn't caught him, but his luck might not hold much longer. If she didn't put him somewhere high and safe then, oversized or no, it would surely only be a matter of time before he become a tasty meal for one of the neighbourhood cats. She had to rescue him. She put down the kettle and, leaning heavily on her stick, hurried out into the hall.

And so it was that, when Lizzie came to the back door, the coast was clear. She peered through the glass and listened for any movement in the kitchen before slowly slipping the key over her head and sliding it into the lock.

May had fumbled with the lock on the front door, the urgency of her mission making her fingers knot and lose their purchase on the catch. As she finally opened the door and stepped out she realised that she had left the keys on the kitchen table. Well, there was no time to go back for them now. She must leave the front door on the latch so that she could let herself back in. She was pleased with herself for realising this before locking herself out. What would Lizzie have said if she'd returned to find May wandering the garden, unable to get back into the house? May smiled a wicked little smile; what would Lizzie do if she knew that May was prepared to go out, leaving the front door on the latch? She'd be absolutely livid! Still much amused at the thought, May turned to negotiate the steps down from the door. In that second, she froze as she both spotted a man coming towards her from the lane and remembered Lizzie's warning note. With a panicked gasp she spun round and pushed the front door open. She stumbled through and hobbled around to shut it behind her. Frantic fingers again knotted, unable to push the latch off. Hearing the man's steps outside the door, she abandoned the attempt and hurried away. Where could she hide? Where should she go? Then it came back to her. She knew where to go and what to do. With renewed purpose she scurried over to the cellar door. She opened the door and went inside, partially closing it after her. Behind her, the man was peering around the open front door.

Steven had seen the old lady hurry away through the cellar door. He'd obviously frightened her, which was strange because Mr Pierce had said Miss Atwell would be expecting him. Perhaps the old girl was a bit senile and had forgotten he was coming. Self-consciously speaking softly to allay the old lady's fears, he walked over to the cellar door and eased it open. It was very dark, with only a weak light in the cellar below. Steven took a step inside, crunching something brittle and broken underfoot as he did so.

"What the heck?" he muttered, confused and unable to

see what was scattered on the floor.

He took a further step towards the top of the stairs.

"Miss Atwell?" he ventured, "Miss Atwell are you down there. It's me, St-"

In a sudden flurry of activity May lurched forward out of the shadowy recess behind him and poked at his back with her stick. Crying out in surprise, Steven stumbled forward to the very edge of the top step, his arm flailing in an attempt to regain his balance. Just as he was about to fall forward, someone grabbed at his sleeve, pulled him back and steadied him. Lizzie had heard him and opened the cellar door. For the merest fraction of a second, she hadn't grasped what she was seeing but, as soon as May pushed at the young man, Lizzie had reacted, only just in time.

Steven fell back against the wall, clearly alarmed.

"What the hell d'you do that for?" he shouted.

Lizzie couldn't think of any excuse for May's behaviour, so she played for time.

"I'm sorry, Steven. It is Steven isn't it? What happened? Are you all right?"

That Lizzie knew his name seemed to calm him somewhat, though he maintained a wary eye on May, who was shuffling behind Lizzie.

"She...I think she pushed me."

He seemed uncertain, seeing May's frail, hunched form in the light now coming in from the hall. He looked from May to Lizzie.

"Are you Miss Atwell?"

"Yes, I am. And this is my sister, May."

Steven did not seem inclined to greet May who, for her part, kept her eyes downcast.

"Are you alright?" Lizzie asked him again.

The young man let out a deep breath, regaining his composure. He nodded.

"Yeah. Yeah, I'm OK."

"Oh, that's good. Then perhaps you'd like to come out now," said Lizzie in her brightest voice, "and I'll show you where we need the locks fixing?"

He hesitated briefly, casting another cautious look at May. Then he nodded again. Keeping Lizzie between himself and May, he edged back out into the hall.

Before Lizzie could follow him out, May tugged at her arm.

"Lizzie, what are you doing? Why did you stop me?"

Lizzie looked down at her sister and didn't recognise the person she saw. Why was May acting like this? Lizzie was at a loss for words.

Again May tugged at her sleeve, her eyes pleading.

But Lizzie was shaking her head; not knowing what to think.

"Go to your room and stay there." she ordered, "I'll speak with you later."

She shrugged off May's hand and went back out into the hall, letting the door close behind her.

Alone, in the darkness, May shrank back against the wall, bewildered. Why had Lizzie protected the prowler? Had she taken leave of her senses? Was she still suffering from that bump on her head? May wrestled with Lizzie's bizarre behaviour for several minutes more, until eventually her whirling thoughts settled. Shamed and sorrowful, she had finally to admit to herself that it was far more likely that she, rather than Lizzie, had acted inappropriately. Yet again she must have confused things; misunderstood and misread the situation. She shook her head in a state of complete incomprehension.

What was going on? What was happening? Who was that man?

12

As instructed, May stayed in her room. She remained there for most of the rest of the day, only moving to go to the bathroom, and once to the parlour while Steven fitted the lock on her own bedroom window. Lizzie brought her a sandwich for lunch and kept her supplied with drinks, but said very little. And similarly, though May wanted to ask questions about this man, she was willing to take her cue from her sister and limited her conversation with Lizzie to nods of thanks.

Steven worked throughout the afternoon and May could hear Lizzie chatting easily with him, discussing household security, the weather, Mr Pierce and much else besides. May was astonished. She hadn't heard Lizzie so voluble for years. Since Frank, Lizzie simply didn't talk to people like this. Why was she chattering so freely with this man? Who was he?

Late in the evening, his work done, Steven made his farewell to Lizzie and departed. The long afternoon of breezy chatter with Lizzie and an amiable meal of tea and cakes shared with her in the kitchen, had successfully overlaid and obscured his memories of May's bizarre behaviour on his arrival. Before he had set to work Lizzie had spoken with him and implied that May was easily confused and timid, nervous of anything out of the ordinary. She hadn't meant him any harm. At first Steven had been loathe to accept Lizzie's version of events, but later, several hours removed from the incident, he had all but dismissed it as the result of his own clumsiness, stumbling about in the dark. Lizzie had been so sympathetic and friendly that it was impossible to believe that he had ever been in any danger here in her house.

Lizzie waved Steven on his way and then closed and locked the front door. Only then did she let the rictus smile slip from her face. Her facial muscles actually ached from the effort of hours spent maintaining a passable semblance of interest in the rather dim young man's conversation and tedious observations on life. She was utterly exhausted and the urge to sleep was overwhelmingly intense. Could she possibly put off till the morning the conversation she knew she must have with May? She dearly wished that she could, but knew that sleep would be impossible if she didn't at least make an attempt to fathom May's extraordinary reaction to Steve. She knocked on May's door and told her to come to the kitchen then waited for her, seated, grim-faced, at the table.

After a short while, May appeared at the kitchen door and stopped, waiting for permission to enter the room. Irritated, Lizzie nodded brusquely. They sat on opposite sides of the table and there was a prolonged silence between them, during which Lizzie stared at May and May avoided her gaze by staring down at the tablecloth. Eventually Lizzie broke the silence.

"Well? What have you got to say for yourself?"

"I'm sorry." May mumbled, almost inaudibly, earnestly hoping that a simple apology would be enough.

"That's it?" demanded Lizzie, "I'm sorry? That's the best you can do?"

Not for a second had Lizzie stopped staring fiercely

across the table and May could almost feel her sister's anger burning into her own downturned head. She thought it wise to continue to stare down at the table.

There was a sudden smack, as Lizzie slammed her open hand down on the table.

"Look at me May! Look at me!"

Startled, May sat bolt upright, eyes wide and fixed on Lizzie.

Lizzie's voice was low and icily patient.

"I'll ask you again. What were you doing in the cellar?" This time she was clearly expecting a full explanation, she spoke slowly, "May, what were you doing?"

Tears were overflowing and slipping from May's eyes. She sniffled noisily, but Lizzie appeared not to have noticed her distress. She didn't even offer May a tissue, but sat, impassive, expectant. She would have her answer.

Suddenly, without composing her thoughts in any way, May spoke.

"I thought you said he was the prowler", she blurted out, "and I wanted to stop him."

Lizzie hadn't expected this. She looked genuinely surprised.

"When did I say that Steven was the prowler?"

"In your letter."

"What? You read my letter? How dare you! You weren't supposed to read that unless something happened to me. And anyway, I wrote that before I'd even heard of Steven. He's not the prowler."

"No, not that letter," said May, still sniffing, "the note you left here on the table."

Still unsure, Lizzie shook her head.

But May persisted.

"You said the prowler would try to come back today and you were going to kill him."

"What! Don't be ridiculous. I said no such thing. The note was just to let you know that Steven was coming to fit the new locks today, in case he got here before I got back from the shops."

"You went shopping?" said May weakly.

"Yes, of course I went shopping. It's Friday. Why? Where did you think I'd gone?"

"I ...I didn't know. I was frightened."

"That's as maybe," said Lizzie, her tone softening a little, "but, for pete's sake, what made you think I wanted to kill him?"

May felt in her pocket for the crumpled note and unfurled it on the table, smoothing it as best she could. Reading it now, the note was clearly innocuous. Lizzie had merely said she would deal with him as, of course, she had always dealt with any handymen and tradesmen who came to the house. May's tears were very now real; tears of embarrassment and guilt. She had made a complete fool of herself and, she paled to think of it, she had nearly killed that poor young man.

Lizzie leant over and proffered a much-needed handkerchief.

"May?"

May nodded.

"He said you tried to push him. Is that true?"

May continued staring vacantly down at the note, saying nothing.

"May?" Lizzie asked again, "Did you try to push him down the steps?"

"Yes." May whispered.

"Why? What were you thinking?" Lizzie, frowned in disbelief, "If he had been the prowler he'd certainly have been ready to kill if someone had just pushed him down some stairs. You'd have just made matters worse."

"He'd have been dead." said May flatly.

"Don't be ridiculous." Lizzie snorted, "He wouldn't have been dead just from a fall down the steps into the cellar."

"He would." May was stubborn.

Lizzie paused. She didn't like this obstinacy. She raised an eyebrow.

"He might have been hurt, I grant you that." she said, her tone patronising and a mirthless smile playing on her lips, "He might even have broken some bones, but he would probably still have been able to pull himself back up the stairs. And then what would you have done? Run to town for help?"

Her mean smile broadened at such a ludicrous mental image.

"He would have died," May insisted, "maybe not straight away, but he'd have died soon enough."

"And you're the expert are you?"

"Are you?" May snapped back, irritated by Lizzie's condescension.

There was a moment's awkward silence. Lizzie was not used to May talking to her in these tones. She wasn't enjoying the new experience.

"If I were you," she hissed unpleasantly, "I'd watch that tone in your voice. You'd do well to keep on the right side of me. And you'd better just hope that I managed to smooth things over with Steven, or you might just get a visit from the police, once he tells them how you tried to push him down the cellar steps."

May's eyes widened.

"D'you think he will say anything Lizzie?"

Lizzie shrugged. She was actually quite certain that Steve wouldn't say a word to the police or to anyone else for that matter, but she was beginning to feel again that wonderful thrill of power, so she decided against immediately reassuring her foolish, trusting sister.

For so long Lizzie felt her life had been constrained by her duty to care for this silly woman; May's needs and wishes had blighted Lizzie's life. She was due some amusement. And though, intellectually, she knew it to be an unworthy desire, she nevertheless wanted to savour this feeling; draw it out, luxuriate in it. She watched as May again lowered her head towards the table and began to rock from side to side in fearful apprehension. So detached was she from May's distress that Lizzie had to struggle to suppress a laugh. She acknowledged only the tiniest nagging prick of guilt at her own behaviour and that weak cry of conscience was easily smothered by her enjoyment of this delicious baiting game. She was at a distance removed from this sad little domestic scene: once more an amused observer rather than a participant. Lizzie was enjoying May's plight but was also mildly sympathetic to it, if only in a detached, godlike manner. Her face wore a satisfied smile.

May looked up from the table unexpectedly, giving Lizzie only an instant to snap back to reality and compose a sorrowfully disapproving look on her face.

"Do you, Lizzie?" May prompted.

"Do I what?" asked Lizzie, frowning.

May was offended by Lizzie's inattention, but continued meekly enough.

"Do you think he'll tell the police?"

Lizzie pretended to think on the matter a moment.

"He might." she said, consciously transforming her look into one of deep concern, "We'll just have to hope that I managed to reassure him, won't we dear?"

This was glorious! The power of absolute control surged through her. It was the most marvellous, exciting feeling. She had to struggle really hard to mask the feeling but, thankfully, May appeared to have noticed nothing.

"Thank you for trying." May murmured pitiably,

reaching over to touch Lizzie's sleeve.

Unsettled by the physical contact, Lizzie hurriedly withdrew her hand.

"That's alright. Now, go get some rest. We can clear up the glass tomorrow. I presume it was you who smashed the light bulb?"

"Yes, with my stick. To make it dark. I'm sorry."

Lizzie had regained her composure. She reached out and patted May's hand reassuringly.

"Shhh. Don't worry yourself about it any more. I'll look after you. Like always."

May managed a pathetic smile.

"You're so good to me, Lizzie." she said, sniffing loudly, "I really don't deserve you."

'You don't know how right you are,' thought Lizzie, with no small amusement.

Having persuaded May to get an early night, Lizzie sat up for a while at the kitchen table. The tingling wash of power that she had been enjoying gradually dissipated and she became thoughtful, turning over the busy day's happenings in her mind.

She had glimpsed the raw determination in May's eyes as she pushed Steve towards the stairs. May had meant to do him harm, no question about it. She must have been terrified of him to act like that. But, thinking about it now, Lizzie was confused. If May had been so unnerved by the note, why had she allowed Steven into the house? It just didn't ring true. Had May been lying? She'd seemed so genuine this evening. If that had all been an act then May was capable of far greater duplicity than Lizzie had ever imagined. Who would have suspected that May's gentle face could mask such a cunning personality? And how could Lizzie have spent so much time and energy over the years, protecting May from the world when May was apparently as capable of being crafty and deceitful as any you might find out there? Lizzie had always dismissed her suspicions about May's childlike, dependent nature as unworthy jealousies. Had she been wrong so often to ignore her own misgivings? Perhaps not; perhaps there was some other explanation. Perhaps she was judging May too harshly.

Then suddenly Lizzie remembered something May had said, something Lizzie had overlooked at the time. 'Not that letter, the one you left on the table,' she'd said. How could she know about the letter? It had been hidden under the table cloth. When had May found it? Had she read it?

Lizzie rose and hurried to the parlour. She felt under the tablecloth. No, the letter was still where she had left it and, on inspection, it appeared not to have been opened. Could May have found it and returned it to its hiding place, unopened? That didn't seem likely. Lizzie knew that, had she found a letter herself, with her own name clearly written on the envelope, she would have read it immediately, even if it had obviously been hidden from her. She'd have to; it might, after all, contain something important, perhaps relating to May's care and safety. Lizzie would have to disregard the usual courtesies. Surely May would have done the same, if for less selfless reasons? Lizzie had soon convinced herself that May had indeed steamed the letter open, read it and then resealed it, before replacing it under the tablecloth here in the parlour. And Lizzie was furious. Was nothing safe in this house? Could nothing be hidden without someone sneaking around and finding it?

That was typical of May; to be so secretive.

The irony of this condemnation was not apparent to Lizzie, very much back in the here and now of her own tunnel vision and, for the moment, unable to observe from a vantage point outside of herself. She was utterly blind to the double standards betrayed by her criticism of her sister. She was filled with righteous indignation and she would speak to May about it in the morning.

Having walked all round the house with Steven just before he left, Lizzie knew all the windows and doors to be locked. So, still muttering irritably to herself, she stomped off, up the stairs, to her bed.

With the new locks and bolts securing every window and door, Lizzie felt safe in the house once more. After what felt like weeks of disturbed nights, she had little trouble in dropping off quickly into a deep and welcome sleep.

However, she soon found herself in the throws of an unsettling dream.

May was in the dream. She was standing at the top of the cellar steps and the steps went on and on and down and down. May's face was tearstained and manic and it swam about, very close to Lizzie's own. As Lizzie watched, horrified, May's face became that of Michael Lowry. He lifted the poker from the fireplace and pushed at Lizzie. 'You'll die you'll die,' he shouted and, with his harsh voice ringing in her ears, Lizzie teetered on the very edge of falling. She tried to cry out as, almost in slow motion, she began to fall. She didn't hit any treads but she turned slow cartwheels, over and over. The fall seemed to go on and on forever.

Shaking and tearful, Lizzie woke just before her dream-self hit the cellar floor.

Still shivering, she drew up her knees and hugged them. All she could hear was the hammering of her heart. She knew she was safe in her own room, but it was difficult to entirely shake off the fear she had felt just moments before, seeing Lowry's wicked face so terrifyingly close. Gradually, her breathing calmed and she turned on to her side in order to try to get back to sleep. But not, she hoped, to dream that dream again.

With some effort, Lizzie gradually began to slip into unconsciousness until a tiny clicking noise pushed into her mind. What was that? Had it been real or part of a just-beginning dream? Awake now, Lizzie lay still and listened. Nothing. She was relieved; but she knew that sleep would be difficult to recapture now.

She slept only fitfully until just before dawn, when she was again woken by the same sound. This time she eased herself out of bed to investigate, grimacing at the awful squeaking of the bedsprings. Not stopping to put on slippers, she pulled her dressing gown about her and went to the window. She drew back the corner of the curtain and peered out into the gloom. There was nothing visibly out of place and Lizzie had just turned to go back to her bed, when she again heard something.

Downstairs!

Fear clutched at her, chilling her heart. How could anyone have got into the house now that the new locks were in place? She forced herself to move, creeping over to the door, easing it open as quietly as possible. As she crossed the landing on tiptoes, a treacherous floorboard squeaked beneath her. She jumped off the board like a scalded cat and grabbed at the banister to steady herself. She clung to the reassuringly sturdy rail while she fought to control her erratic breathing and mounting terror.

There was another noise downstairs.

Whoever it was, was now in the hall, directly below her. Biting her lip, Lizzie stiffly leant her head forward a fraction, to look down the stairs. She gasped and clasped her hand to her mouth to stifle a scream: Lowry was walking slowly across her field of view. He was heading for May's room!

In that instant, seeing Lowry creeping towards her

sister, a lifetime's conflicting emotions jostled for supremacy in Lizzie's head. Her thoughts of just a few hours ago now seemed unworthy; May was her little sister and she had promised to protect her. Yet Lizzie could not completely dismiss the judgements she had made.

She was torn, her mind divided and in conflict with itself. She both loved and resented her little sister and, while she'd always cherished May's innocence, she now suspected her capable of manipulation and deception. She wanted to care for May, as she had promised Mother, but also bitterly resented the imposed obligation to care. And though she was proud to have looked after May as well as she had for so long, she nevertheless saw her own life as just so many wasted opportunities as the direct consequence of having had to make that commitment.

With all these conflicting feelings, what was it that made her now turn to the stairs and go down to confront Lowry? Was she going down in order to rescue May or did she simply want to get this whole ordeal over, once and for all? In truth Lizzie herself had no idea, but, whatever her motivation, she didn't once consider abandoning her duty or running away from whatever was to happen.

Clutching the banister all the way, Lizzie made a faltering descent to the hall. She was now reconciled to the conviction that this was how it was going to end; Lowry would kill May and then come back for her. She felt weak, almost beyond fear; resigned to the fate she had fought to hold back for so many years. Now that the time had come, she almost felt relief, but she shut her eyes and covered her ears. She didn't want to hear May screaming out for help that she could not give. Her legs buckled under her and she slid down into a hunched squatting position on the bottom step, resting her head against the wall.

She waited.

She waited; but nothing happened. She eased her hands from her ears and opened her eyes. Still nothing. There was no sound whatsoever and nothing seemed out of place. Looking about her, Lizzie could almost believe she had dreamt the whole thing. And this wasn't so far-fetched an idea. Over the years, on the inside pages of the more sensational newspapers she'd read several reports of people sleepwalking whilst having vivid nightmares. True, these stories had usually ended tragically when the sufferer fell out of an upper window, or unknowingly stabbed their partner, but maybe Lizzie had been lucky enough to suffer only a mild form of the condition. Though she hardly dared hope this could be the case and felt she was probably clutching at straws, she began, in the continuing silence, to dare to think that it was a real possibility.

Slowly, she rose to her feet. Still there was silence. She wiped her damp palms dry on her dressing gown, pulled her shoulders back and stood erect. She was feeling in control again and had all but accepted the sleepwalking explanation of events. She had only to check that May was unharmed, to be completely convinced of it. Stiffly, but determinedly, she walked to May's door, took a deep, steadying breath, then gently turned the handle.

To her enormous relief, May was there in the bed, fast asleep and there was no sign of any violence or indeed of anything at all out of the ordinary. There was to be no confrontation with a violent prowler, no traumatic and bloody ending. Lowry had been in Lizzie's own head. She could breath again. She and May were safe.

For now.

Lizzie made her way back upstairs, marvelling at the vividness of the subconscious. Her dream had seemed so very real, in every respect as clear as any waking experience. She shook her head. She had been convinced and would have sworn an oath that Lowry had been here in the house and, thinking back, she couldn't tell at what point she had woken up. In fact, it could be that she was still dreaming even now. Perhaps, when she opened her bedroom door, she would see her real self, asleep in her bed.

Lizzie smiled at this foolishness and yet, when she reached her door, she hesitated for a moment before turning the handle.

13

There was no sleeping self, unconscious in the bed. Lizzie was no longer wandering a sleeping world, a dream-shadow of herself. She was here and now. This was reality.

But when she opened the blinds at her window, she was instantly transported away from reality: spellbound by the sublime, unnatural beauty of the garden below. The world beyond was hidden, engulfed in the thick cold mist of early morning while, within the garden, in absolute silence and stillness, every tree, every shrub and every blade of grass stood pale as ghosts, dusted with tiny needles of hoarfrost.

Perfection.

Light seemed to be coming not only from above but from all around, from within the mist. It was so astonishingly beautiful that Lizzie could only stand and stare. How was it that she had never appreciated this view before? How many thousands of mornings had she looked, without ever seeing, without once experiencing this wonder?

This spontaneous, fresh appreciation of the ordinary and everyday seemed, to Lizzie, to be happening more and more frequently. Once, she would not even have noticed children playing in the school yard; and the terrible, pressing need always to stay alert had formerly excluded any appreciation of glorious weather. But lately, without any warning, Lizzie would unexpectedly find herself seeing, feeling and thinking things as if for the first time; as if she were viewing things from some new and very different perspective. From this changed angle, the familiar would suddenly strike her as something utterly novel and intriguing. After a life busy with the concerns of hard work and responsibility, Lizzie had lately found herself dwelling less and less on the material or the routine responsibilities of her day. More and more she was concerned with her subjective impressions of the world around her.

To less obviously positive effect, Lizzie was also becoming increasingly absorbed by the internal musings of her own head. In the past she had never been much given to introspection, regarding it as an indulgence, a distraction from the necessary daily business to be done. And though this self-awareness was currently an interesting novelty for her, Lizzie had already discovered that she had perhaps been wise to avoid it all these years. Self-awareness had brought with it self-doubt and mistrust. With growing frequency, she was finding herself reflecting on the motives underlying both her own actions and those of others. She kept returning to the serious doubts she had been entertaining about May's character over the last few months. Why, when for so long she had believed her sister to have the perfect innocence of a child, did she now so often find May's character lacking?

It was all most disturbing.

Until all this new vision and inner analysis had started, there had been a large measure of order and certainty in Lizzie's life and, although a constant underlying feature had been the enduring dread of the world outside, the very unchanging predictability of her routine had itself been a comfort to her. She thought perhaps that it was the particular perspective of old age that was producing this move towards introspection. If so, then she could do nothing to prevent it. She had to accept it, albeit with reservations; her old life had been dull and often frustrating but, while this new questioning approach could be intriguing and thrilling, it could also be alarming and disconcerting. The changes had introduced excitement to her humdrum existence, even to this latest experience of lucid dreams and sleepwalking, but, fascinated as she had been by the guilt-free pleasure she had enjoyed in baiting May, Lizzie suspected that the change in her would ultimately deliver only disillusionment and doubt.

In the past, Lizzie had felt this free-fall into uncertainty only rarely and briefly, during the anxious lonely nights in which she struggled with her old dread of the time when death would take her and leave May to face the world alone. But, with her recent tendency towards introspection, the sense of falling over the edge seemed always to be just a short step away. Lizzie had changed and, day after day, she could feel herself changing further.

Even as she marvelled at the loveliness of the early morning garden, she was wondering with some trepidation what other new experiences life was preparing for her.

After dressing, Lizzie went down to the parlour and felt under the tablecloth for the letter. In the reasoning light of day she was no longer so ready to believe that May had steamed it open and read it but, to be certain that it wouldn't be found accidentally, she would need to find it a more permanent hiding place. She stood in the hall, tapping the edge of the envelope on her hand as she tried to decide on the safest place. As before, she faced the problem that it had to be somewhere that May would not happen upon in the normal course of her day. But it also had to be somewhere that May, or perhaps an investigating detective, would find during the thorough search of the house that would result were Lowry to break in and do his worst.

Lizzie still had no sense that she was perhaps being overly dramatic in her thinking: whatever Lowry's motives, if he continued his prowling and managed, somehow, to get into the house and attack her, Lizzie wanted to be sure that her testimony would be heard. It seemed to her that hiding the incriminating letter was simply the obvious, prudent course of action.

Years of reading dire headlines and cliché-ridden crime reports had encouraged her expectation of criminality and harm from the outside world. Every lurid banner headline and graphically described assault had reinforced that expectation, with the result that Lizzie's hugely negative view of the threat she faced was now actually a good deal further from reality than was May's naïvely optimistic outlook.

As Lizzie turned slowly, her eyes searching the hall, she found herself absently trying to recall when it had been that she had started thinking of him as 'Lowry' rather than as 'Officer Lowry', or even 'Michael Lowry'. When did their relationship slip into the use of a familiar, single name?

Her mind thus wandering, Lizzie continued to survey the hall, looking for a hiding place. Her gaze took in the corridor leading to May's room and, at this, her attention refocused on the task in hand. Of course! If she didn't want May to find and read the letter until the time was right, why not put it somewhere she'd never expect Lizzie to have put it: in May's own room? May might not like Lizzie going into her room uninvited, but this was vital for her safety, so Lizzie felt no compunction in ignoring

May's wishes. Indeed, Lizzie was smiling. She was hugely pleased with herself. How amusing it would be to know that the letter was safely hidden, but under May's nose all the time.

She tiptoed along the corridor to May's room and tapped the door very gently; wanting only to check that May was still asleep, rather than wake her. Receiving no response, she turned the handle and eased the door open. Having already decided where to put the letter, she crept past the bed and slipped the letter onto the top of the wardrobe. But, creeping back to the door, Lizzie caught her toe on the edge of the rug and stumbled, knocking into the bed. Roused, May opened her eyes. Still half asleep she stared, confused, at Lizzie who was frozen in mid-stumble, her hand gripping the end of the bed for support. Neither said a word. Inexplicably, May then simply smiled and settled back down on the pillows. Within a few moments, she was again gently snoring.

At a loss to understand what had just happened, Lizzie was nonetheless grateful for it. She waited another full minute, silent and motionless in the half-light, before she crept to the door and out of the room.

In the kitchen, making a pot of coffee for breakfast, Lizzie tried to decide whether May had been awake. May proudly guarded her privacy. Surely, if she had been conscious, she would have demanded to know why Lizzie was creeping about in her room. But she hadn't said a word. She'd simply smiled and gone back to sleep. Lizzie shook her head; her sister was unfathomable.

May woke again several hours later.

Hearing her moving around, Lizzie had quickly to decide how she should explain having been in May's room earlier. Her best option would probably have been to tell May that she had been sleepwalking. Lizzie could have made it sound convincing since it was nearly truthful; she had been sleepwalking, just not at the time when she had disturbed May. But Lizzie was not about to tell May that she had suddenly taken to walking in her sleep while having bizarre dreams. Lizzie would never admit to such unorthodox behaviour. The sleepwalking was her own private business. No one else need ever know.

With little time for creative thought, the best excuse Lizzie could concoct was that she had heard a mouse and followed it to May's room. It sounded unconvincing, even to Lizzie, so she decided not to raise the subject first. Best to wait and see how May felt about her intrusion and take it from there. Also best left till later would be the discussion she would have to continue with May about her attack on Steven. Lizzie hadn't yet decided what, if anything, she should do about May's behaviour. Just thinking about it again brought back all of last night's conflicting emotions. Yes, best leave it a while.

When May eventually came into the kitchen, Lizzie said nothing and waited. May, however, was her usual self, cheerfully asking if there was any more coffee in the pot. Lizzie mumbled that she would make fresh. She was still waiting for May to make some reference to her being in her room. Surely May would ask for some explanation?

But no. She sat and drank her coffee, thanking Lizzie for making it and chatting happily about nothing of consequence.

"That was a lovely cup of coffee, Lizzie. Thank you." she said at last, "I'll just make up the dough for some bread then I'll go pick the vegetables for our soup. Would you like anything in particular?"

"No. I don't mind. Anything is fine."

While May mixed and kneaded the dough, Lizzie slowly washed the cups and coffee pot. She loved to watch May making bread. Like their mother, May made the lightest, most delicious bread and, for Lizzie as an observer, the whole process of its preparation contributed hugely to the enjoyment of the bread itself. Lizzie had been taught how to make bread, but hers had never been as good as May's and for years the task had almost always fallen almost exclusively to the younger sister. Not that May resented it. She loved the smells and warmth of home-baked bread and she took quiet pride in the praise it earned her. With stray seeds from the nearby fields drifting into her garden, May had even taken to growing some cereals herself, to add her own personal touch to the mix.

As Lizzie watched, May put the dough into the small loaf tin, dampened a clean cotton cloth and stretched it over the top. Then, opening the oven door to warm the air, she left the dough to rise. As May wiped the flour from her hands, she looked up and smiled at Lizzie. Lizzie found herself smiling in return. It was the smile of a shared moment of contentment and satisfaction in a job well done. No words were needed and, if May did harbour any lingering irritation that Lizzie had earlier disturbed her sleep, she didn't let it show on her cheerful face.

For her part, May now decided to grasp the opportunity afforded by Lizzie's rare good humour to ask her a favour.

"I wonder, Lizzie, would you do something for me?"

"It depends; what do you want?"

"There's a book in Father's study. Could you get it for me please?"

"I suppose so. What book is it?"

"I can't remember the title exactly, but it's a book about moths."

"Oh, for pete's sake!"

"Please, Lizzie. It's sure to have a picture of the

Polyphemus in it and I'd love to show it to you. I think if you saw it you'd understand."

"Don't go raising your hopes. What does it look like?"

"It's warm russet in colour and it has the most amazing eyes on the wings."

"The book, May. What does the book look like?"

"Oh, I see. Sorry dear. It's a large book, bound in dark red leather. It always used to be on one of the high shelves."

With the little good humour she enjoyed evaporating fast, Lizzie went to search for the book. It was, as May had described, on a high shelf in one of the book cases. It was also dusty and smelt slightly of damp. Lizzie dragged it down from the shelf and called to May.

"I've found it. Where do you want it?"

"Could you bring it in here please, Lizzie?"

"Sir, yes, sir." Lizzie muttered.

With the huge book spread open on the parlour table, May pleaded with Lizzie to stay a while and read it with her.

"I have work to do, May." Lizzie protested.

"Please Lizzie, after what happened this morning, I really want you to see this."

Was this an oblique reference to Lizzie being in her room and waking her this morning? How irritating: Lizzie had just come to believe that May must have been asleep. Now she'd have to apologise and Lizzie hated to apologise. She took in a breath and prepared herself.

"Look, I'm s-"

But May interrupted.

"Shhh Lizzie, please just a few minutes. Please."

Lizzie gave in. She supposed that looking a few pictures of a moth had to be better than making an apology.

"Alright. Show me."

May hauled the book closer and slid the thick, glossy pages over, looking for the Polyphemus.

"Here it is! Look, Lizzie."

Lizzie glanced across with little interest, but found her attention caught and held by the illustrated plate on the page. Painted as if it had just settled on the paper, the impressive, life-size image was of a huge orangey-brown creature with wide, feather-like antennae and what appeared to be fur on its powerful, stocky body. Its impressive wingspan was at least five inches tip to tip. But May had been right; its most amazing features were the 'eyes' on its wings. Huge, dark-lidded eyes looked out balefully from the partially closed hind wings. To Lizzie's eye, the overlaid hind wings created the semblance of a nose while below, completing the 'face', was a slash of black and pale pink, which ran across both hind wings like a wickedly smiling mouth.

Lizzie shuddered.

"It's horrible."

"Horrible? What ever do you mean? He's magnificent."

"To you, maybe. To me, it just looks evil. An evil, grinning face."

May was baffled at so visceral a response. Lizzie wasn't normally someone who spoke of fanciful notions. Describing the Polyphemus as evil-looking seemed entirely out of character.

"I'm sorry, Lizzie, I'm afraid I don't see it."

Lizzie pointed to the overlapping wings and the darker line below.

"Look there's the nose and there's the mouth."

May laughed.

"But Lizzie, it only looks like a face because the wings happen to be overlapping in that picture. If the wings were farther apart then there wouldn't be a nose or a mouth, would there?

"There are thousands of different types of moth, with different patterns and colourings and they come in all sizes. They're every bit as interesting as butterflies. And, you know, one thing that's always intrigued me is the way moths fly. They do flutter, but they seem more purposeful than butterflies, more powerful somehow. I think it must be because they're nocturnal and attracted to light. We can see exactly what it is that guides them. We know where they're going; there's an understanding between us. But if you watch a butterfly it flutters up and down, up and down and who knows where it's heading? We don't know which flower its aiming for and it might just as easily fly up and out of the garden altogether.

"Moths are truly wonderful creatures. And, the 'eye' markings are only there to protect him from predators, Lizzie. Mind you, he's so big now that I doubt he could be threatened by anything."

Lizzie pointed to the illustration.

"Your moth is bigger than that?"

"Oh yes, much bigger. And he seems to be getting even bigger by the day."

"Wonderful." said Lizzie, expressionless.

"Yes it is." said May, apparently failing to recognise Lizzie's sarcasm, "Of course, his being large is quite appropriate isn't it?"

"Appropriate? Why?"

"Come now, I'm sure you remember your Greek stories."

Lizzie looked blank.

"Polyphemus was the son of Poseidon, remember?"

"What's that to do with being big?"

"He was the cyclops."

"Who? Poseidon?"

Lizzie was teasing her now and May looked cross.

"Polyphemus was the cyclops. In the Odyssey. You do remember don't you? He captured Odysseus and his crew on their way back from Troy."

"Yes, yes, I know. But I also seem to remember that he ate some of the crew."

May nodded.

"Let's hope your huge moth doesn't do the same."

"Oh really, Lizzie." May heaved the book shut, "I thought you'd be interested."

"Why would you think that? I've never been interested in your moths before. Why would I start now?"

"Because this is an exceptional specimen, Lizzie, quite exceptional."

"Yes? Well I can't see why it's named after a cyclops. The cyclops only had one eye and Odysseus poked that out, so he ended up with no eye. But your moth has the two huge eyes on its hind wings as well as the two little ones on the other wings. It doesn't make sense to me."

"Yes, well it does to me." said May sharply. "Please leave the book here. I might want to look at it again later."

"Oh yes? And what are you going to do now?"

"I told you before: I'm going to get the vegetables."

May shuffled to the kitchen. Lizzie followed. May took down the new key from its hook, unlocked the door and went out onto the verandah.

Lizzie watched from the window, as May stiffly descended the steps to the lawn and crossed to the vegetable patch. Though Lizzie was relieved not to have had need to use her implausible mouse chasing excuse, she was baffled. Did May have any recollection of Lizzie creeping around her room and waking her up? She'd seemed to hint at it, but had demanded neither an apology nor an explanation.

'She's a strange one' Lizzie thought, shrugging.

She knew that May had a capacity to put things out of her mind, but surely, not something odd, that happened only a few hours ago? Yet that is exactly what May appeared to have done. No explanation required. Nothing. The incident might never have happened.

'Strange.'

Walking the rows of plants in the vegetable patch, with the joy of warm sunshine on her back, May was feeling similarly relieved not to have had a difficult talk with Lizzie.

After going to her bed early yesterday, at Lizzie's insistence, May had been restless and, having tried to sleep for several hours, without success, she had eventually gone to watch her beloved moths. Her initial intention had honestly been to stay inside, watching the insects through the window, as Lizzie had wanted. However, this was not out of any delayed acquiescence to her sister's wishes, but only because May had forgotten that a new lock had just been fitted on the kitchen door.

However, once in the kitchen, May had found the new key. Delighted, she dressed hastily and went out onto the verandah. The night was chill but, with her rug over her knees, she was quite cosy and soon the moths had worked their usual magic on her. She had to confess that the experience was made even more enjoyable by the knowledge that she was again triumphing over Lizzie's unnecessarily overprotective rule. May no longer felt any guilt for having disobeyed Lizzie on the evening when she had lost the key while she was out watching moths. She had tried to apologise for causing Lizzie so much trouble, but Lizzie had refused to accept her apology and had reacted, May thought, with quite unnecessary rudeness, calling her a selfish woman. Having spoken so harshly, Lizzie had then sulked up in her room all that afternoon.

But, sitting out on the verandah, watching the moths, all that unpleasantness with Lizzie was forgotten and May was blissfully content. Everything was fine until the time had come to go back in. Stiff from sitting still for so long, May had been clumsy, making worryingly more noise than she would have liked in returning to her room. She was sure that she must have disturbed Lizzie and had expected a grilling this morning. But Lizzie had said nothing. Perhaps Lizzie had slept better now that the new locks were in place. Well thank goodness for that!

It had felt good, once again, to have the freedom to go out; to feel herself no longer a prisoner, locked inside the house. And May's enjoyment had been crowned by another visit from the Polyphemus.

After such a wonderful night, May had overslept this morning, but Lizzie hadn't made a comment about that either.

'Strange.'

Both sisters approached their meeting again at lunchtime with a degree of trepidation. Had they just been lucky to get away without an awkward argument this morning, or had sufficient time now passed to consider the matters closed? In working together to prepare the vegetables, they were carefully polite to one another and they chatted amiably enough as they cooked the soup. They then sat down to eat their meal in silence, having by now exhausted all the possibilities for small talk arising from the morning's chores. Soup was slurped and spoons scraped noisily on dishes.

Lizzie began to find the noises irritating, while the lack of conversation left her mind free to dwell on the concerns she had been having about May. Maybe now was the time to get some answers to yesterday's nagging doubts. First, she wanted to ask May why she'd let Steven into the house if she'd really been so frightened by Lizzie's note.

But how to start?

She decided to lead up to her real questions circuitously and perhaps catch May off her guard.

"May?" she asked, "Did you remember to clear up the broken lightbulb?"

May stopped, soupspoon halfway to her mouth. She looked completely blank.

"Lightbulb?"

'I don't believe it' thought Lizzie, 'she's forgotten already.'

Aloud, she said,

"The one you smashed with your stick. Yesterday."

May frowned.

"You remember," Lizzie urged, "you broke it so that the top of the cellar steps would be in darkness."

May was beginning to look distressed, shaking her head.

"You wanted it to be dark," Lizzie continued, "so that you could hide in the shadows and push young Steven down the stairs."

"No."

"Yes you did."

"I don't remember."

"I think you do. You told me yesterday that you were so frightened that you tried to push him down the stairs."

May's face was frozen.

"Do you remember now?" asked Lizzie, "You do, don't you?"

There was a brief pause, then May's answer, which was no more than a whisper.

"Yes."

Lizzie eased herself back in her chair.

"Well, what I want to know is, if you were so frightened, why did you let him into the house?"

Again, May looked confused. She hadn't pushed the boundaries of her memory back to the point of Steven's coming into the house. She didn't remember letting him in. She remembered...she remembered trying to close and lock the door. Yes, she was trying to lock the door...to stop him coming in, but she couldn't get the latch off. She'd remembered to put the latch on so she wouldn't be locked out. She'd been pleased with herself that she'd remembered before she went out, but it didn't seem so clever now, in the light of what had happened afterwards. So, she had been outside. But why? The moth. Yes, it was coming back to her; she was going out to rescue the Polyphemus. She remembered it all now. But May hesitated, not wanting to tell Lizzie that she had been about to go out leaving the front door open, on the latch.

"Come on." Lizzie insisted, "Why did you let him in?"

"I didn't."

"Yes, you did. He told me that you left the door open for him. How else could he have got in?"

To May it seemed that it would be her word against Steven's. Surely Lizzie would believe her version of events rather than that of a stranger.

"He was lying." she said boldly, "Perhaps he broke in."

Lizzie was staggered at the weakness of her sister's grip on reality.

"What? Why would he break in?" she demanded, "He was coming to fit the new locks. No one breaks into a house when they know the householder is going to be in and waiting for them."

May winced. That had been silly, she could see that now. She tried another tack,

"I thought that maybe you'd let him in when you came back from the shops."

"How could I?" Lizzie snapped, "I came in by the back door."

As soon as the careless words were out of her mouth Lizzie tensed, expecting an outburst of anger from her sister. But May didn't react. She hadn't grasped the implication of Lizzie's admission. She wasn't really listening. May was preoccupied, struggling to find an explanation for yesterday's events that would not further provoke Lizzie. But, finding no such explanation, she decided just to tell Lizzie the truth, or at least as much of the truth as proved necessary.

"He got in because I couldn't get the door shut quickly enough. I'd been outside." she said, "But not far from the door." she added hastily, "Honestly."

Lizzie was unsure what she was being told.

"Are you saying that you went out and left the door open?"

"Not open exactly," May explained, "on the latch."

"You left the door open?" Lizzie continued, ignoring May's interruption, "How many times have I told you?" She snorted, shaking her head, "But of course you don't listen, do you? You never do. How many times have I told you? You must never leave the door open when you go out into the garden."

She was angry but she didn't expect an answer and May merely shrugged.

"Always, always lock the door behind you when you go out."

"I didn't have the front door keys." May started, but then remembered, "Oh yes I did, you left them here for me didn't you? Oh Lizzie, I'm sorry. It won't happen again."

Lizzie let her head sink onto her chest. She was

exasperated. There had been no enjoyment, no sense of power during this exchange, only anger and weary disappointment. She had been deluding herself in thinking that she ever had any real control over May, or her actions, because May so rarely listened to anything Lizzie told her and never followed any of her advice. It would be no surprise to Lizzie if Lowry were to come back to the house and find the newly fitted locks left wide open by her foolishly unconcerned little sister. There would be no need for him to break in, because he had May doing her idiot best to ease his way into their house, to wreak havoc in their lives.

May would one day leave the door wide open for him and he would come in and that would be the end of them both. Stupid, silly May would be the death of them!

In bitter frustration Lizzie clenched her fists, scrunching the material of her skirt. She fought to keep her voice level.

"You have to stop doing this. May? Are you listening to me?"

May nodded, eyebrows raised at all the fuss Lizzie was making. Fortunately, Lizzie hadn't notice the disinterested look heavenwards.

"For the last time," Lizzie continued, "it's not safe to go out and leave the door open. In fact you shouldn't go out of the house at all when I'm not here. Do you understand what I'm saying?"

Again, May nodded.

"Then say it!" Lizzie demanded.

"Yes, I understand."

Lizzie relaxed a little, until May continued,

"But not if it's an emergency of course. It would be alright for me to go out then wouldn't it?"

"No!" Lizzie shouted, her patience completely blown away, "You just stay in the house. Understand? You stay in the house. End of story."

"End of what, dear?"

Lizzie wanted to scream, but was choked by the tension gripping her throat. Her head was pounding with the effort of trying to reason with May. Her tightly clenched fists were shaking. She had to calm down. She had to go somewhere away from May and calm down.

"I'm going to my room." she said curtly, already on her way out of the kitchen.

"Good idea," said May indulgently, "you have a nice lie down."

14

While Lizzie stayed in her room over the next few hours, May pottered around in the garden, enjoying the fine weather. After the little unpleasantness over lunch, she had taken care to lock the kitchen door but, not wanting to risk losing the key again, she had then used a length of green garden string to tie the key to the door handle. It would be safe there until her return.

She came back in, tired but satisfied, having worked hard to catch up on some of the jobs that had remained undone over the last few days. She felt she had earned a rest and perhaps a small treat, so she poured herself a small glass of ginger wine and took it through to the parlour. Easing herself into her favourite armchair, she took a sip of wine and steadied the glass on the tiny side table then, shaking her handkerchief from her pocket, she dabbed at her eyes, clearing them before taking up her knitting needles. She was hoping that there would be a pretty sunset this evening. That would be the perfect end to a lovely day.

Lizzie came down and crossed the hall, heading towards the kitchen. Out of the corner of her eye she saw a small movement in the parlour. She froze, then carefully turned back to check. It was just May sitting waiting for her sunset. Lizzie stood a moment, watching her sister. She wondered whether, like her, May had spent the hours since lunch worrying about their future, trying to remain calm in the face of uncertainty and the threat of Lowry's return. Looking at her now, clicking away with her needles, contentedly oblivious, Lizzie concluded that she probably had not.

May was truly blessed with her forgetfulness. All of life's troubles could be shelved and forgotten, leaving her to enjoy a wonderfully carefree existence. Lizzie wondered what went on in May's head. Was she aware that she was continually discarding large chunks of her past? Again, probably not. She certainly didn't have the look of someone bent low with worry.

May looked up, smiled and said, "Hello there."

But she didn't seem at all offended when Lizzie walked away, choosing not to reply. Lizzie did not forget things so easily and she was in no mood to talk.

Lizzie made herself a sandwich and a cup of tea and, normally, she would have offered to make the same for May, but she did not. She was still angry. What made the anger harder to bear was the fact that May had obviously already put the whole lunchtime argument behind her. Lizzie wanted there to be some recognition of the frustration she felt. There should be tension in the air, with May nervously waiting to see if Lizzie had forgiven her. Instead, May was knitting. She was comfortable in her favourite armchair, a glass of wine at hand, knitting.

Lizzie's sense of grievance was building. She wanted to hit back in some way; she wanted to break down May's insufferable complacency. To this end she decided to demonstrate her annoyance by taking her food through to the parlour and eating it in front of May while, pointedly, not offering her anything. It was a plan worthy of a silly and petulant child, but Lizzie chose to ignore this; in the manner of an affronted would-be duellist, her sense of injustice demanded satisfaction.

At first, May appeared not even to have noticed Lizzie. This was irritating, but Lizzie countered by stirring her tea with excessive noise and an exaggerated clattering of spoon on saucer. May finally looked up, blinking, from her knitting.

"Are you eating something, dear?" she asked, dabbing at her eyes to see more clearly.

Lizzie ignored her. But, far from being upset, May merely smiled.

"That's right. It'll do you good. Enjoy it."

Then she returned to her knitting, completely unconcerned. That was too much for Lizzie. Snatching up her plate, she strode out of the room.

Behind her, the knitting needles clicked and clacked in mocking laughter.

Lizzie now paced the kitchen, muttering furiously. May was absolutely maddening! How could she just sit there, totally unconcerned, while Lizzie ate and drank right in front of her and didn't even offer her so much as a sip of tea? And how typical it was of May to be so self-absorbed that she hadn't even noticed that Lizzie was in the room. Lizzie had been driven to making quite a lot of noise to get May's attention. And when, at last, May had stopped pretending that Lizzie didn't exist and looked up, she'd smiled for God's sake. She'd said, 'Enjoy it.'

"Enjoy it!" Lizzie spat the words.

The adult calm of May's response in comparison to her own childishness, was a further irritation to Lizzie. She didn't want to act like this. She could see that it was unworthy of her...but she just had to wipe that smile off her sister's face. Lizzie couldn't bear to think that May had somehow got the better of her.

Perhaps she should go for a walk to cool off. Yes, she'd try that.

Marching out of the kitchen, she snatched up the bundle of house keys from the hall table and rammed them into the pocket of her cardigan. She pulled at her coat on its hook by the door, but the coat wouldn't come. Lizzie tugged at it violently. With a nasty ripping sound, the collar of the coat split open and the garment fell into Lizzie's hand.

"That does it! That does it!"

In a fury she threw the coat to the floor then with nothing planned, but her temper still boiling, she marched back into the parlour and directly to the window. She wrenched the blind down but it leapt back to life, rattling straight back up again the instant she let it go. Livid with rage, Lizzie made an inarticulate noise deep in her throat. She snatched at the pull cord and dragged the blind down again, repeatedly ramming it down to its farthest extent, all the while snarling and spitting complaints at the unfairness of her life.

Still seated only a few feet away, May refused to be a part of this nonsense. She would not allow herself to see it, and would ignore it until it stopped. Throughout the entire performance May serenely continued with her knitting, apparently oblivious to Lizzie's manic behaviour.

Finally Lizzie began to tire and had to moderate the force of her pull. The blind now stayed in place, but Lizzie was exhausted.

"For the last time; pull the blinds down after dark." she hissed through clenched teeth.

That got a reaction from May. With ostentatious calm she folded her knitting away and smiled.

"Hello dear." she said placidly, "Did you enjoy your snack?"

Lizzie could stand it no longer.

"Will you stop that?"

"Stop what, dear?"

"That 'sweet little sister' act. You're not fooling anyone."

May raised an eyebrow.

"I don't know what you mean," she said testily, "I asked a friendly question, nothing more."

May paused until she had regained her calm.

"You know, Lizzie dear, I think we should both get an early night. Things always seem better after a good night's sleep."

"I'm staying right here." Lizzie growled.

"Well, perhaps you'll excuse me then. I've had a long day and I'm ready for my bed."

May gripped her walking stick and started to rise, but Lizzie put her hands on May's shoulders, forcing her back down onto the chair.

"Lizzie!" May gasped, shocked at this rough handling.

Lizzie bent forward so that her face was only inches from May's.

"You're going to stay here with me," she hissed, "until you answer some questions."

Now May was angry too but, for the first time, she was also a little afraid of Lizzie. She shuffled in the chair, tugging her cardigan to her and freeing herself from Lizzie's grip with a feisty shake of her shoulders.

"What do you want to know then?" she asked, impatient to get this unpleasantness over with.

But Lizzie was still shaking with angry indignation. She needed to calm down before she could begin to argue cogently and, having finally got May's full attention and willingness to answer her questions, Lizzie also realised that her questions were too numerous. She had been asking herself questions for so long that she couldn't now put them into words to have them all answered.

She wanted to know if May was really as foolish as she had always seemed, or was that pretence? And if May was really as simple as she acted, how was it that she was able to use those fancy words of hers? How was she able to memorise all those facts about hundreds of moths? And how was it that she could recall detail from Greek myths learned in childhood while apparently completely forgetting what had happened only hours before? Lizzie wanted to know if May had ever understood the warnings and instructions she had given her over the years. If she had, then why hadn't she acted on any of them?

Finally Lizzie needed to know whether May actually cared for her at all, or had just taken advantage of her sense of duty all these years. Lizzie had always tried to believe the best of her sister; she had to know if that belief had been misplaced. If May's whole personality, the apparently childlike innocence, the lack of guile, had all been a sham, then Lizzie's life too had been made a sham, a pointless waste.

In truth, Lizzie wanted her life justified and, May was the only person left who could supply that justification. But it was a lot to demand of a few questions.

"Well?" May prompted, still indignant. She wanted to go to bed and instead she was being made to sit here, waiting, while Lizzie paced back and forth, saying nothing.

Lizzie appeared not to have heard May's question, but she knew she had to start somewhere. Right. She would begin by trying to sort out what had happened yesterday. If May had put any thought into her attack on Steven, if it hadn't just been a panic reaction, then surely that would be proof of an ability to plan and to act independently, that went far beyond May's usual capabilities.

"May," she began, "do you remember what we were talking about at lunchtime?"

May sighed, casting her mind back to that disagreeable little talk they'd had. It had quite ruined her enjoyment of the soup.

"Yes."

"You said you'd been outside."

"Yes. I went out to rescue the moth."

"Rescue it from what?" Lizzie asked, beginning to take a slight interest, in spite of herself.

"Well, it's grown really huge and it seems to walk, instead of flying and I thought it might get attacked, by a cat or something, if it stayed on the ground. So I was going to put it up somewhere high."

"How?"

"Sorry?"

"How were you going to get up anywhere high?"

Until this point, Lizzie had been inclined to believe that May had indeed gone out after the moth, but this was ridiculous. With the arthritis in her knees May had difficulty in walking. Climbing was out of the question.

"I know. Silly isn't it?" said May, smiling weakly, "But I hadn't actually thought it through."

Lizzie gave May an appraising stare. She might be telling the truth. She might be inventing the whole lot. May's facial expression lent nothing to either possibility.

"Did you get the moth?" Lizzie asked, "Where is it now?"

"I didn't get it, but I know it's alright."

"And how do you know that?"

"Because I've seen it since then; yesterday evening and again today. And it was in the house again today. Oh I wish you could have seen it Lizzie. It's a beautiful creature and so sociable. I feel that it knows me now. It comes to visit me and I must admit, I talk to it."

"Does it talk back?" asked Lizzie flippantly.

May sniffed and dabbed at her eyes.

"No, Lizzie. The moth does not talk back."

Lizzie shrugged.

"You say this monstrous insect has been in the house? How is it I've never seen it?"

May eyed her sister carefully. Was she going to be serious now? Could she actually be interested in the moth? It seemed unlikely, but May had such lack of success in the understanding of motives that she couldn't be sure. She sighed.

"I don't know." she said, "It seems to have accepted me. It may take a little while before it becomes accustomed to your presence."

'Accustomed to your presence!' thought Lizzie, 'There she goes again; a simple 'gets used to you' would have been enough for anyone else. But not for May.'

"And you don't think it's at all strange," she then said, aloud, "that I have never seen this huge moth of yours?"

"What, never?"

"No. Never. Not once. Neither inside nor out. Not a single, solitary sighting of the thing."

May looked guarded. She didn't like Lizzie's tone.

"Well, yes. I suppose that is a little strange."

"More than a little, I'd say. Tell me about it."

"What?"

"Tell me what's so interesting about this damn moth."

"There's no need to speak like that Lizzie. I'll tell you if you're really interested, but I don't think you are. You just want to poke fun at me. I don't know what's gotten into you today."

"No, you're right, I couldn't care less about the thing and, if it exists, I daresay I'll see it in the flesh soon enough."

"What do you mean, 'If it exists'? Of course it exists."

"It doesn't matter," said Lizzie off-handedly.

"It does matter. It matters very much." May

countered indignantly, "Do you think I'm lying about it? How dare you! Why on earth would I lie? It's utterly ridiculous."

"I didn't say you were lying, just that it was strange that I've never seen this moth and yet you're seeing it all the time, even inside the house. After all, you did tell me that it's very large, for a moth. Hard to miss, I'd have thought. In my place, wouldn't you think it odd that you only claim to see the thing when I'm not with you?"

"I don't like your tone and I don't like being questioned in this way. And if you think I've lied to you then why are we having this conversation at all?"

'Good question,' thought Lizzie.

"And, anyway," May continued, "you're just the same; you keep telling me you've seen Officer Lowry everywhere..."

"And?"

"Don't you think it's odd that I've only ever seen him when he came, in his police car, just like a proper policeman. Whereas you keep seeing him sneaking around the garden."

"And in the house."

"What?"

"Nothing."

May was thrown for a moment, but quickly recovered.

"You see," she continued, "I might just as easily wonder why it's only you that sees the prowler."

Lizzie was furious. She stopped her pacing, right in front of May.

"May, are you calling me a liar?"

"I would never use such an ugly word, anymore than I trust you would of me."

Stalemate. They faced each other in frosty silence. Lizzie was first to break away. She turned and restarted her pacing of the room as she spoke.

"OK," she said, "forget the moth." she paced a few more strides, concentrating, "Yesterday, you told me that you couldn't get the door shut in time to stop Steven coming in. Is that right?"

May sighed and looked sullen. She made no reply.

"Is that correct?" Lizzie asked again.

"Yes." said May crossly.

"So he was hot on your heels was he? You must have been terrified."

"I was." said May, shuddering at the memory, "I was absolutely terrified."

"And you had only seconds to find a place to hide."

May nodded.

"And yet you had enough time and were able to think clearly enough, to get to the cellar door and smash the lightbulb with your stick so that it would be in darkness. And then you knew to wait for him to follow you in so that you could push him down the stairs. That was some very quick thinking, May."

May frowned, bemused. What was Lizzie getting at? What did Lizzie want her to say? It had all happened, but she'd had time beforehand to decide what she should do.

"I'd read your note in the kitchen, so I had time to plan what I'd do if the prowler came before you got back."

"Mmm, that's true. But, what a thing to plan; you said you thought the fall would kill him."

"Yes."

"In fact, you were convinced of it."

May said nothing.

"You kept saying, 'He'd be dead. He'd be dead.' What made you so sure?"

Still May said nothing. She dabbed at her watering eyes, to little effect.

"You see," Lizzie continued, "I find it more than a

little odd that my normally placid, day dreaming little sister planned to ambush Steven and push him down the stairs to what she believed was certain death."

May's lip was trembling. Seeing her, Lizzie began to feel again the wonderful thrill of power. May was cowed and Lizzie was back in charge. 'Ignore me, would you?' Lizzie thought, 'You won't make that mistake again.' She stopped pacing and came over to sit in the second armchair, opposite her sister. She eased herself comfortably down and relaxed, watching May sniffling and dabbing at her tears: a pathetic sight.

Lizzie savoured the moment.

"Still nothing to say?" she asked.

There followed several minutes of silence broken only by May's occasional sniffling. Lizzie was enjoying being back in control of the situation. A momentary recollection of her earlier childishness, in eating the sandwich in front of May and the memory of her explosive battle with the window blind, brought Lizzie some brief embarrassment, but she reasoned that her behaviour had been understandable. She couldn't have let May carry on as she was, being so unconcerned, so disinterested, and so rude. May had ignored her, simply to anger her. Lizzie's own behaviour, on the other hand, had been thoroughly excusable. Unavoidable really. It had unfortunately been necessary to be rather unkind to May in order to try to shake her up a bit.

During this spell of quiet, May was also thinking.

May had known that Steven would be killed if he had fallen. It hadn't just been a belief. She had known it. She turned her mind back to yesterday. She had read Lizzie's note and had known what to do. How? Where had her plan come from? As May concentrated, the older, buried recollections slowly came back into focus. She was reawakening memories that she had kept hidden for decades. Her face relaxed and became still, her eyes focussed not on anything in the room around her, but on events that had happened a lifetime before. Though her hand continued to dab at her eyes from time to time, the action was now completely automatic, requiring no conscious thought: May's mind was preoccupied, elsewhere.

What had happened all those years ago had been awful, but it had been an accident. May had only meant to stop him but something had gone wrong and she had kept the secret from everyone, even from herself, ever since. Everyone had always thought of her as a silly, gentle and frivolous child, to be protected and cherished. And that was how May had wanted it. She tried always to be kind and cheerful, courteous and sweet and she had buried her disturbing memories deep in some dark secret corner of her mind. No one had ever known what she was really like.

And now, after all these years, it seemed that Lizzie no longer believed the disguise. Somehow Lizzie had seen through the mask, the appealing exterior, to the substance beneath; so there was no reason for May to pretend any longer.

May's attention returned to the present. She looked up and caught sight of Lizzie's gloating smile, before Lizzie had a chance to suppress it. May was confused. Why was Lizzie so pleased with how things had worked out? Lizzie couldn't yet know what May had done all those years ago or she wouldn't have been smiling. She was sure to be distraught when she found out, but now that Lizzie had seen through the veneer, there seemed little sense in keeping the secret any longer. May would have to tell.

Lizzie looked across at her sister with distaste. May was so weak that it was sometimes difficult to believe she really was her sister. May was clearly hiding something about yesterday's events but, given time, Lizzie would find out what that something was. She suspected that May had said something embarrassingly silly to Steven, or acted foolishly or perhaps she'd been cowardly and now didn't want Lizzie to know about it. Lizzie was intrigued. But how to get May to talk?

She had an idea.

"I spent a lot of time yesterday, talking to Steven." she said, matter-of-factly.

May looked up.

"Yes." Lizzie continued, "He told me everything that you said and did. He said he thought I ought to know."

May's face was a blank. She was utterly mystified. She hadn't said a word to Steven and she'd already admitted trying to push him, so what more could Lizzie be talking about?

Lizzie was a little disappointed at the lack of response, but she persisted.

"So you see," she continued, "there's no need to be so secretive. I know all about it. But I would like to hear it all in your own words."

May was shocked. Had Lizzie read her mind? How else could she know that May had a secret? Did Lizzie know everything? Had she known all these years? Surely not: no one could have been as good to her as Lizzie had, if they'd known all along what sweet little May was really capable of. But if not that, then what on earth was Lizzie talking about?

"Lizzie, I don't know what to say." said May hesitantly.

"Just tell me what happened, in your own words." Lizzie coaxed, controlling her impatience with great effort.

"You want me to tell you my secret?" May sounded unsure.

"Yes, in your own words." Lizzie replied, inwardly

delighted at how little effort it had taken to get May to tell all.

"Are you sure you want to know?"

"Yes I'm sure. I mean, as I said, I do already know. But it would be better to hear it told in your own words."

"Very well," said May quietly.

For May, after a lifetime, the opportunity had finally come to unburden herself. Though she had managed, for most of the time, to bury the events and the guilt associated with them, they had always been there, as gaps in her memory, among the first of many blank holes in her past.

After all this time, May was ambivalent about telling Lizzie. On one hand, she had kept the secret for so long, that the very keeping of it had become a part of her and would be hard to put aside; but, on the other hand, if Lizzie took it well, it would be marvellous to feel herself loved even though her true nature was known. But then again, if Lizzie did not take it well, which seemed the more likely outcome, there could be no taking the words back. The secret would be out for good.

May twisted her handkerchief between her hands as she wrestled with her indecision. Her face was set in the deepest of frowns.

Watching her, Lizzie was becoming weary of May's prima donna performance. Why didn't she dispense with all the preliminary wringing of hands and the agonised looks and simply spit it out? It was so typical of May; a touch too extravagant and self-indulgent. After all, whatever had happened yesterday surely couldn't have been that bad. Why was May making such a fuss?

Finally May spoke.

"When we were children, I used to idolise you Lizzie. Did you know that?"

Lizzie was taken aback. What was this? What had their childhood to do with anything?

May continued, wiping away a tear.

"I always wanted to join in your games and play with you, but you were older and you didn't want a baby sister running after you. You used to hate it when Mother made you take me with you. Do you remember?"

Lizzie nodded hesitantly: agreement without understanding.

"I grew up trying to be just like you. I even wanted to dress like you, in those awful dungarees. Do you remember?"

Again, Lizzie nodded, her frown deepening.

"I used to watch you all the time, even when you were older and you and Frank would sit out on the verandah for hours just talking, talking, talking. I must say I was envious of the closeness you two had. I could see how very much he meant to you."

Lizzie was now staring at May, but not making a sound. It was rare for May to talk about Frank. Lizzie had always supposed it was because he was nearly twelve years older than May, the baby of the family, so she had never known him the way Lizzie had. A tear slipped down Lizzie's cheek as she suddenly realised that she hadn't thought of Frank at all today. And yesterday she'd been so occupied dealing with that silly young man and trying to stop May injuring him, that she'd also forgotten him then. She could not excuse herself. Though she had been busy with other, pressing concerns, Lizzie felt she had betrayed Frank, not his memory but him personally, by passing a whole day without calling him to mind. It had never happened before. Frank was a part of her life everyday and always would be. How could she have been too busy to remember him?

More tears were falling now.

May continued in her quiet, even voice.

"Then, when I was thirteen or so, Frank must have told Mother and Father that he was going to marry Vera. No one told me what was going on of course, but I remember you running upstairs and slamming the door. You cried for hours into the night and I couldn't understand what could possibly have upset you so much. Do you remember? We had to share the room then and I thought something terrible must have happened, but I couldn't ask you. When Mother told me, the next day, I must admit I was glad he was getting married. You see, I thought you'd have more time for me once he'd left home. That was horribly selfish of me wasn't it? Lizzie?"

May paused. She had dabbed at her own eyes and could now see the tears on Lizzie's cheeks.

"Are you alright Lizzie? Should I stop?"

Lizzie, still silent, shook her head.

"Very well, if you're sure." May continued, "Where was I? Oh yes, as I said, I was pleased at first, but then I realised how devastated you were by the news. And it only got worse when we actually met Vera. I was watching you at that meal, when Frank brought her here to meet us, and I could see how appalled you were. You tried to hide it and no one else seemed to notice, but I knew. I could tell. You thought she was awful. And you were right: she was absolutely awful. You hoped that Frank would see the mistake he was making, didn't you?"

Lizzie nodded.

"You see," continued May, "I could tell. And it hurt me to see how miserable you were. But, of course, Frank didn't see sense and he married her. I was so worried for you on their wedding day, I thought you might do something silly. Don't forget, I was still young and given to rather fanciful notions. I'd read about tragic heroines committing suicide over a lost love and I really thought there was a risk of that with you.

"When they got back from their honeymoon and they stayed with us for a few months, I remember things weren't so bad because you still got to see him everyday. But, when they found a home of their own and moved out, it was pitiful to see how much you missed him. It broke your heart didn't it?"

Lizzie's nod was barely perceptible.

"I never really forgave Frank for upsetting you the way he did in marrying that woman. I had hoped that you and I might become close, so maybe you would feel able to confide in me. I hoped I'd be able to comfort you. But, of course that never happened. You were a grown woman, helping Mother and caring for Father in his final illness. I was still just a child, someone else you had to care for. We would never be friends or equals and I had to accept that. I tried to be a friend to you though and I used to help when I could. You didn't know, did you, that it was me who would set the table or hang out the washing or sweep the hall rugs, while you were busy elsewhere? It was me, not Mother. Sometimes I would hear you telling her that she was overdoing things, that she was trying to do too much and she kept telling you not to worry, she was fine. And all the time it was me. I liked to pretend I was your magic helper, doing the work secretly, like the fairy story of the elves and the shoemaker. I loved and admired you so much that I didn't need any thanks or recognition.

"And things just carried on like that. Then Father died and, for a short time, Frank and Vera stayed with us, after the funeral, do you remember? It was while they were with us that it happened."

Lizzie wiped away the tears with her hand.

May continued.

"You'd gone into town with Mother and Vera and I

195

was up in my room. Frank was fixing a shelf in the bathroom. He'd just finished and was putting the hammer and things back into the tool-box when I came out of my room. It was getting dark so he hadn't seen me, but I could see him and I could tell he was unhappy. He looked so sad that even though, as I said, I was angry with him, I asked him what was wrong. I thought he must have been thinking of Father.

"But he said he was sad about something else. He said that Vera wanted to move south because the cold winters made her ill. I forget where it was he said they were going, but I know it was hundreds of miles away. He said that Vera had a weak constitution and needed a sunnier climate. But I could tell that he didn't want to go so far away, especially so soon after Father's death. But even though he didn't want to go, he had applied for a new job there and he'd been told he was almost certain to get it.

"And all I could think of was how sad you were going to be when you heard the news. And I was furious with him for not standing up to Vera and refusing to go. He said that I didn't understand; that it was complicated. But I understood alright and I was so angry that I shouted at him for being such a coward and leaving Mother and you when you needed him most.

"I thought I'd be in terrible trouble for talking to him like that, but he didn't say anything. He just sort of shrugged. I told him he'd been a fool to marry Vera, that she was a selfish, controlling woman. And he didn't even tell me to be quiet. I wanted a reaction. I wanted him to say something. I thought that, if I could get him to argue with me, there was always a chance that I might be able to persuade him to stay. But he wouldn't argue. He wouldn't say a word.

"He packed away the last of the tools and took up the box. I followed him. I was still telling him what I thought he should do. I was so rude to him, Lizzie. I was horrible. I said everything I could think of to convince him that he was wrong, but he just looked sad. He didn't defend himself at all."

Nodding through her tears, Lizzie whispered, "He would never have argued with a child. He was a strong man, a leader, but he was gentle."

"I know that now," said May, "but then I just thought he was weak. I was really angry and so frustrated at his passivity that I did something stupid. Lizzie, I pushed him. Not hard, just to get a reaction really. But he was right at the top of the stairs and he fell backwards, head over heels, all the way to the bottom.

"I was screaming and, when he didn't get up straight away, I was sure he was dead. I ran down to him but he was unconscious. He'd taken a nasty knock on the back of the head and, as I watched, it started to bleed. I ran and got a cloth and some iodine from the cupboard to clean the wound and it was only after I'd done that that he began to recover. I kept telling him how sorry I was and he told me over and over that it was alright, 'No harm done.' I put a folded cloth under his head and stroked his forehead while he recovered. We were there, on the floor in the hall for ages, until he was able to get up."

Lizzie was looking puzzled,

"I don't remember this," she said.

"No." said May, "By the time you all returned, later that evening, Frank was back on his feet and I had put away the tools and cleared the blood off the floor in the hall. He'd put on his hat to hide the lump on his head and he told all of you that he and Vera had to leave earlier than expected. He didn't say anything to anyone about what I'd done and he promised me that he would go home to rest and call out the doctor immediately if he felt poorly.

"Before he left he told me not to say anything to you or Mother about his moving away: he wanted to tell you himself. But he never got the opportunity to tell you did he? He had his brain haemorrhage two days later. He died and I killed him."

15

The room was silent.

May was exhausted, slumped back in her chair. Lizzie was staring, uncomprehendingly at her.

There was nothing more for either to say to the other.

The two women grew cold, sitting so still, while around them the sun sank a bloody red and the room gradually darkened. Eventually May was roused by an exceptionally violent shiver.

"I do feel better telling you after all this time." she said, her voice a dry whisper, "Are you alright, Lizzie?

Lizzie briefly raised her eyes to May's and then let them sink back down again, tacit affirmation, though she said nothing and remained, otherwise, absolutely still. May was concerned. She leant forward and bent lower to try to see up into Lizzie's face.

"Please say something."

But Lizzie didn't look up again and merely shook her head by way of reply. She didn't know what she felt about what May had told her. She was struggling just to take it in. With so much going on in her head Lizzie couldn't connect with May in any way, not even eye to eye. She didn't want to look at May's face and certainly was not ready to talk yet. Lizzie would have to grapple with and understand her own feelings first.

After a moment's indecision, May grasped her walking stick and hauled herself upright. She swayed unsteadily, her cold, stiff limbs complaining. Normally, Lizzie would automatically have put out a hand to help her, but now she sat inert, no sign that she had even noticed her sister's struggle for balance. May leaned on her stick and made a tentative first step. Her knee locked painfully, but she knew that the second step would get easier. She walked slowly and carefully to the door then turned her head, intending to wish her sister a good night. However, the sight of Lizzie's hunched form stayed the words before they were spoken.

May turned away and left the room.

May had gone to bed but, unusually for her, was having great trouble in quieting her mind for sleep. She felt the lifting of a burden in having at last told someone her secret. She no longer had to wear the mask; nevertheless, she couldn't say that she was happy. That feeling of relief and contentment was in abeyance, awaiting Lizzie's acceptance and forgiveness for the terrible wrong she had done her in taking away her beloved brother.

Lying in her bed May tried, but could not dispel the image of Lizzie, silent and motionless in her chair. She hadn't heard Lizzie going up to her bedroom so she supposed she must still be sitting in the parlour.

How small and vulnerable Lizzie had looked, sitting there, all alone.

Then May's mind began to turn back over her memories of the evening. As she did so, the seated, pitiable image of Lizzie gradually gave way to the memory of Lizzie as she had been earlier in their conversation, when she'd had the upper hand. As the mental image changed, May's feelings for her sister also changed, from pity to fear. She felt again the withering disdain that Lizzie had poured into her voice as she had spoken, asking May questions that had left her confused and upset.

'She didn't believe the Polyphemus had been here at all,' thought May, still smarting from Lizzie's implied accusation of deceit. True, May had lied through omission these many years, banishing many painful or upsetting memories from her conscious mind, but she was proud that she always strove not to tell lies by commission. She knew the moth was real. It was certainly very much larger than was usual, but it was real. She had seen it clearly, many times. It had visited her. And it did appear comfortable in her presence. Why had Lizzie found that so hard to believe? Why did she think May would lie about any of it?

The loss of Lizzie's trust was not something that May could endure and, having now told Lizzie about Frank, May's greatest fear was that she might never regain it. She faced the likely prospect of a future in which Lizzie would always treat her with the cruel, taunting disbelief that had so upset her this evening. What could she do to heal the mistrust between them?

It occurred to May that, if she could prove to Lizzie that she had not lied about the Polyphemus, Lizzie would see that she was truthful after all. Lizzie might then be willing to have faith in her once more and, in time, might even come to forgive her for Frank's death.

May resolved to capture the moth and show it to Lizzie. There could be no arguing with the evidence. Lizzie would have to believe her. But, how to capture the creature without injuring it? At length May remembered the large roll of muslin that her mother had bought years before and from which she had cut covers for her jars of preserves. There would be plenty left on the roll and it would be perfect for the job. It would be light enough to cover the moth without damaging its magnificent wings. She decided to get it from the kitchen first thing tomorrow.

But as time went by and it became clear that sleep was not going to gather her up though she was quite desperate for rest, May decided to abandon the wait and go in search of the muslin straight away. She liked the sense of purpose; setting herself a task helped her mind to focus. Perhaps a spot of physical activity was what was needed to help her mind to clear itself sufficiently for sleep.

She eased herself out of bed, pulled on her dressing gown and, cane in hand, shuffled along the corridor towards the kitchen. As she passed the parlour door, she glanced in. Thankfully, Lizzie was no longer sitting there.

'She must have gone up to her room after all,' thought May, much relieved.

But the chair was not empty. As her eyes became accustomed to the dark May could make out, there, on the arm, the familiar form of the Polyphemus. Her first thought was that it might have finally shown itself to Lizzie and she might therefore already be convinced of its existence. That would be wonderful but, as a precaution, May decided she would persevere with her attempt to capture the beautiful creature.

As quietly as possible, she edged back, out of the room.

The old roll of muslin was down on the floor of the larder, tucked away under the lowest shelf. With a tremendous effort May managed to clear heavy glass storage jars out of the way and drag the muslin into the middle of the floor. It was covered in twenty years or more of dust and cobwebs and she could see now that moths or some other pests had made several large, ragged holes in the delicate cloth. It would not now be of much use as a net to capture the Polyphemus.

But May was desperate to prove the moth's existence to Lizzie. She was no longer even sure why it mattered so much. She only knew that it did.

Still undecided as to how she was going to capture the moth, she made her way back to the parlour.

Lizzie had remained in the parlour for a long time, devastated by what May had told her, that Frank might be alive today had May not given way to a childish fit of anger. Lizzie had used those stairs every day of her life, never knowing what had happened there. Now she pictured her beloved brother falling over and over down those very steps, a rag doll with its life being shaken from it. Trying to erase the image, she shook her head. Tears were pouring down her cheeks.

Were it not for that instant of dreadful temper and stupidity on May's part, Frank might have been there through all the dark times in Lizzie's life, helping her and dispelling the terrible loneliness she had endured through the long years without him. How could she ever forgive May for that?

Lizzie reached back to the awful day when Henry Fisher, their doctor and family friend, had come here, to this house, with the news that darling Frank had died just an hour before. He said that Vera had called him, but it had been too late to do anything for Frank. He had died quickly and peacefully, Dr Fisher assured them, as a result of a haemorrhage in his brain. Lizzie had stood in the hall, frozen in shock, supporting her mother who was already crying out and weeping inconsolably. Unlike her mother, Lizzie had been unable to cry then. She couldn't make any sound. Her mind had simply stopped, utterly unable to absorb what she had been told. She remembered that the doctor had carried on talking. Yes, he had even asked if Frank had had any falls or bumps on the head lately. She remembered shaking her head, dumbly.

Then the doctor had taken her mother from her, into the parlour. Lizzie had been left all alone in the hall.

And she had been all alone ever since.

That action of May's, just an instant, one second in a whole lifetime, had changed Lizzie's life forever.

And how was she to explain May's behaviour since that dreadful day? Was the fact that May had successfully hidden her guilt for so long, the sure proof of Lizzie's suspicions? Did it prove that May was indeed both clever and manipulative and had played her older sister for a fool her whole life. Or, just beneath the surface, was May still that scared young girl, horrified at what a moment's flash of temper had caused? Had her apparent simple-mindedness arisen from a need to block out a frightening incident in her past?

Lizzie turned the possibilities over and over in her mind, but could not resolve them. For all her search for the truth, she still had more questions than she had answers. She wanted to believe that her life of caring had been a noble sacrifice, not a misguided folly. She wanted to believe that May was good. Once she had rested, she would have to speak to May and she fervently hoped that she would find some reason to excuse and to forgive her.

Eventually, exhausted, Lizzie slept.

May was back at the parlour door, hardly daring to hope that the moth would still be there, on the chair. It was! Now, how to catch it? She scanned the room but could see nothing suitable: no vases or containers large enough to hold the moth safely until the morning. She drew nearer to the chair, her eyes fixed on the moth. The insect started to become restless. If May couldn't find something to use to trap it soon, it would fly off and who knew when she might see it again? She must catch it now. She had to show the proof to Lizzie tomorrow. Then Lizzie would know that she wasn't all bad; she wasn't someone who told lies. She wasn't like that.

Desperation led May to think the unthinkable: if she couldn't catch the Polyphemus alive, then she resolved to kill it. She simply had to have the proof. But what on earth could she use to kill it? She'd never killed a moth before: she watched and studied, but had never collected. She had seen photographs of moth and butterfly collections, where the poor creatures were pinned out for display. But this moth was too big for that. An ordinary pin wouldn't go through it. She would need a nail or something.

Of course!

May sidled over to her chair and began slowly to unroll her bundle of knitting. She drew out one of the long, sharp needles and moved cautiously back towards the moth.

After a welcome hour or so of sleep, Lizzie stirred. She wasn't fully awake but she knew that there was someone in the room with her. She slowly roused herself, absently tidying her hair; a quick fluttering of the hands. She opened her eyes.

It was Lowry!

Suddenly fully awake, Lizzie's mind reeled in total confusion. What? How? What was he doing here? How had he got into the house? The locks, they were supposed to keep him out. Oh god, what was he going to do?

Though her mind was in shock, Lizzie's muscles leapt

into action and she sprang up out of the chair. Her heart was racing, her whole body trembling. She backed away from him, eyes fixed on the wicked knife he was wielding.

He followed her, saying nothing, his movements slow, deliberate. Lizzie wanted to scream at him to get out of her house, but her throat had so tightened with fear that she could not. She turned to run, her mind focused on getting to the knife drawer in the kitchen. She had to arm herself.

Expecting at any second that he would grab at her, she fled into the hall. At the door to the kitchen she risked a look over her shoulder. He was just coming out of the parlour, following her, but he moved slowly, stalking her. A predator, he was going to take his time.

He was in control.

As Lizzie turned away again, she caught her foot in the sleeve of the coat that she had earlier dumped on the floor. Frantic, she stumbled into the kitchen, trying to shake the thing off.

"Damn it!" she shouted, finally finding her voice.

She kicked off the coat and went to get the knife.

May sighed.

The moth had fluttered quickly away before she could catch it. She was still thinking of what she was going to do in terms of 'catching'. She didn't like to dwell on the real task she faced, that of killing this beautiful, trusting creature. But she knew it had to be done.

Then she heard Lizzie, presumably woken by her antics. And Lizzie didn't sound pleased. If she was awake, she'd be down soon. May had to find and catch the moth before she appeared. She had to be able to prove to Lizzie that she had been telling the truth. She simply had to.

Knitting needle in hand, May hobbled after the fleeing Polyphemus.

Lizzie was at the knife drawer, but it was empty. Where were the knives? She scanned about her in terrified panic. Lowry was already in the room. Anguished, Lizzie finally caught sight of the knives. They were all where they had been left, ready for washing. But Lowry was now between her and the sink. And he was moving closer.

Lizzie could now do nothing but back away.

Suddenly she stumbled and fell backwards her hands flailing wildly. Her left arm smacked sharply against the larder door and she hit the tiled floor with a loud crack. Bones had broken. Her hip, her leg? She couldn't tell. The pain was excruciating and yet, still on her side, Lizzie managed to drag herself away from Lowry by pulling on the table top with her good right hand.

He was still coming for her, slowly and silently, stalking her around the kitchen table.

Without taking her eyes off him, Lizzie felt above her head, along the edge of the table top, for something, anything with which to defend herself. Her searching fingers nudged something. What? Some sort of cloth. Angry, frustrated, she flicked the useless thing away. Her fingers scrabbled painfully along the edge. What was this? Something metal? Frantically she straightened her back, wincing and gasping with the pain, straining her neck to get her head to the level of the tabletop. For a second she looked away from Lowry, to the thing in her hand. A spoon! She let it go and desperately scanned what little she could see of the table. From her low perspective, a pickle jar loomed large but out of reach and the discarded tea towel lay crumpled near her panicking eye, blocking much of her view. There was nothing useful within reach, nothing sharp or heavy. Lizzie started to whimper, tears of frustration stinging her eyes.

She knew she was going to die. She knew, but she was powerless. It was happening just as she had feared all these years. Finally all the bad in the world that she had tried for so long to keep at bay had caught up with her and she was completely helpless against such evil. She went limp with despair and only her steadying hand on the table top stopped her collapsing completely.

She looked up at his cruel face, blinking back the tears. He was holding the knife above his head. He held it still, grimacing with the effort, but he didn't move or make a sound.

Sobbing, Lizzie begged for her life, "Please, please no."

But her pleading brought no mercy. He brought the blade down, its vicious point ripping through her hand and deep into the wood of the table.

May had held her breath. It was there. The moth was clambering about on the furniture right in front of her. She heard Lizzie call, but she didn't respond. She had to do this first. She had to get it, pin it down so it couldn't escape again. For a few moment she held the needle above her shoulder, silently dreading what she had to do. Then, closing her eyes at the last second, she slammed the knitting needle down into the moth's soft body. She had it! Lizzie would have to believe her now. The pathetic creature was jerking, pinned to the table, liquids oozing from its collapsed and broken body.

May called to Lizzie to come see it,
"Lizzie! Lizzie!"

Lizzie was in agony and deep in a hopeless misery, yet still she found herself angered that this monster had used her name. He had called her, mocking her with it.

It was a final cruelty. It made this so premeditated, so personal. It gave him more power over her. Why was he torturing her like this? Why didn't he just finish her off?

Lowry leant down towards her, his head very close to hers. She followed his eyes. He was looking at her skewered hand, fascinated. He was silent again and so close that she could feel his breath on her face, but he seemed almost to have forgotten her, interested only in her hand. He moved to wrench the knife out of her hand. Her eyes widened. What was he going to do now? She'd read many times of killers who keep gruesome trophies of their victims, an ear perhaps, some hair. Was he going to cut her hand right off?

"God no." she gasped.

Unaware of Lizzie's desperate struggle, May was looking closely at the moth. It had not died. It was still twitching. She wished it would stop. She wished it would just die quickly.

There was a sound, very close.

Who said that?

Apparently startled by Lizzie's gasp, Lowry hesitated for a moment and Lizzie seized her opportunity. With a huge effort she wrenched the bundle of keys from her pocket and stabbed their cold jagged mass into the unprotected side of his face. His skin tore and peeled open.

Suddenly, out of the corner of her eye, May saw

something flying at her. Another moth? Perhaps it was trying to protect its mate or maybe trying to avenge it. All she knew was a terrible pain as the second creature repeatedly cut and tore at her face. She couldn't believe the force of its attack. Her face was burning. Hot blood was running down her neck.

Lizzie swung back and stabbed again. Blood spurted and flowed down Lowry's face, filming over his eyes and bubbling at his mouth and nose. In vain he tried to blink the blood away and blindly flailed his arm at her. But Lizzie was in a frenzy. With heedless strength overcoming her terrible pain, she was ferocious. She couldn't let him go. She couldn't let him go on to attack May. She had to stop him. Again and again Lizzie swung the bunch of keys at the man's bloodied head.

Her strength was fast draining away, but she had done enough. Lowry was struggling. He staggered backwards and fell almost at once, tripping over Lizzie's broken leg. Unbearable pain crashed over her and she slumped in a faint, her body trailing like a length of heavy drapery from the table top, where her hand was still pinned to the red sodden wood. Her head and the rest of her body lay as an awkward crumpled mass on the floor.

In terrible pain and blinded by the blood now pouring from the wounds on her face, May stumbled and fell to the floor. Her head smacked against the floor tiles, cracking her skull. There was an instant's awareness of searing pain, then she knew no more.

Spreading and rolling, lifting tiny whorls of dust and

carrying them along on its darkly shining, scarlet skin, May's blood fingered its way slowly across the floor of the now silent kitchen, to pool and mingle with that flowing from the piteously broken body of her unconscious, dying sister.

16

Two weeks later, a policeman acting on a call from Miss Willets at the library, bumped his patrol car along the quiet lane and parked outside the house. Unable to raise any response to his hammering on the front door, he searched the garden then worked his way around the house, checking windows and doors. Nothing seemed out of place or in any way unusual, until he rounded the back of the house. He stepped up onto the verandah and rattled the back door handle. The door was locked and didn't open, but it did give sufficiently for him to be aware of the throbbing buzz of insects and the overpowering foulness of the air within the room beyond.

He was young, but an experienced officer and he was in no doubt as to what he was likely to find inside. But he had been to this house before and he felt he owed it to the old ladies to be sure that there was nothing he could do to help them. Tying a handkerchief over his mouth he repeatedly threw his weight against the door. Finally, the door gave way and he spilled into the kitchen.

It was as he had feared. There was nothing to be done.

Swallowing hard to quell his turning stomach, he stumbled out of the house. He called the incident in from his patrol car then sat for a while, door wide open, breathing in deep, welcome tides of fresh air. But he couldn't stay there. He had a duty to those old ladies: he should at least keep watch over them until the rest of the team arrived. It was a pointless act of protection and care but, though the ladies were beyond any help, he could not do otherwise. He couldn't leave them alone, like that. He stood up, straightened his uniform and went back up to the house.

Soon other cars rolled up. Officers and investigators came to the house and relieved him of his post. He went back to the station to write up his report.

He had written many such reports before and was well used to the expected approach: the document should be comprehensive, factual and couched in scrupulously detached language. But the young police officer had been touched by this case: the elderly sisters had reminded him of his own elderly aunts and his grandmother. All these ladies had belonged to a different age, a slower, more genteel past that had now slipped away forever.

He detailed his findings and documented the appalling scene, the bloody result of terrible violence, but young Officer Lowry ended his report on a rather wistful note.

His concluding sentence read that, as in life, so in death: these two devoted sisters had remained together, even to the last.

Acknowledgement

I'd like to thank my husband and children for their encouragement in my writing, with special thanks going to Alex for his excellent proof reading (any remaining slips will be due to my later additions). I'm also extremely grateful to my publishers ;-) I can't thank Peter enough for his unfaltering confidence in me; it has turned the long and sometimes difficult process of bringing my story to the printed page, into an exciting adventure and a lot of fun.

Alison Buck, March 2006

Alnpete is an exciting, innovative new independent publisher.
Watch out for the next title from Alison Buck:

Abiding Evil
Alison Buck

A sleeping menace is roused deep in the darkness of the forest. For decades it grows, biding its time, reaching out to tug at the ordinary lives of those living beyond the shadow of the trees.

Their children begin to disappear.

Unaware and unsuspecting of the danger, a group of families, friends for many years, journey to a newly opened hotel. It stands alone in a clearing a mile or more within the forest boundary.

For some this will be their last reunion.

Coming Summer 2006 ISBN 0-9552206-3-7

Visit the Alnpete Press website www.alnpetepress.co.uk
for the latest information on our titles, authors and events

Alnpete is an exciting, innovative new independent publisher.
Check out the first Peter White mystery from Simon Buck:

Library of the Soul

a Peter White mystery

For years the CIA have been using a poison designed to cause a heart attack and then disperse without a trace. Now a batch has gone missing.

On a visit to Rome, Peter White is recruited by his old friend Costanza into the oldest secret society in the world, in order to help her solve an urgent problem. Cardinals and other clerics around the world are dying of unexpected heart attacks. Police authorities are not interested as there is no evidence of foul play. But Costanza believes someone is using electronic cash and a betting website to fund and coordinate a campaign of murders that will ultimately lead to the assassination of the Pope. She and Peter must track down the killer before any more people die. Using the world's largest supercomputer, deep in the Secret Archives beneath the Vatican Library, they lay an electronic trap and wait. But when the Library itself becomes the target of an audacious plot to steal a 2000 year old manuscript, the problem suddenly becomes much more personal.

Available now ISBN 0-9552206-0-2

Visit the Alnpete Press website www.alnpetepress.co.uk
for the latest information on our titles, authors and events

Throughout a science-biased education and subsequent years employed in graphic design and web site development, Alison Buck has all the while been scribbling away, committing her stories to disc. Although, as a rule, she concerns herself with apparently quite normal, everyday characters, populating what appear to be quite normal and everyday surroundings, the events and dangers they encounter are rarely commonplace; Alison's can be very dark, unsettling tales.

But whatever the origin of these often menacing undercurrents in her stories, Alison assures us that they are completely at odds with the happy and relatively menace-free family life she enjoys with her husband, son and daughter in Kent.